HAPPY IN THEIR LOVE

Men of the Border Lands 10

Marla Monroe

MENAGE EVERLASTING

Siren Publishing, Inc.
www.SirenPublishing.com

A SIREN PUBLISHING BOOK
IMPRINT: Ménage Everlasting

HAPPY IN THEIR LOVE
Copyright © 2013 by Marla Monroe

ISBN: 978-1-62740-248-4

First Printing: June 2013

Cover design by Les Byerley
All art and logo copyright © 2013 by Siren Publishing, Inc.

Printed in the U.S.A.

PUBLISHER
Siren Publishing, Inc.
www.SirenPublishing.com

HAPPY IN THEIR LOVE

Men of the Border Lands 10

MARLA MONROE
Copyright © 2013

Chapter One

Abraham Waverly cursed as he climbed back up the bank of the river. The fishing equipment alone was enough to unbalance him as he crawled over rocks and maneuvered around stumps without the added weight of the fish he had caught. He'd be damned if he lost any of it or took a header into the river. It had taken entirely too long to catch the damn things.

Finally the ground leveled out enough he could stop and rest a minute. He still had a good twenty-minute hike to make it back to the lodge, and it was getting to be late morning already. Normally, it didn't take as long to catch a few fish if he got there early enough, but for some reason, they'd been harder to catch than normal.

"Probably getting late enough in the year to have them seeking deeper channels," he muttered to himself.

Abe knew it was somewhere around the middle of August from the shorter days and temperature changes. He'd been living there for about the last seven years and had long since stopped trying to keep up with the days of the week and the months in the year. All that mattered was following the signs to know when to plant the garden or bring the cows closer to the lodge. He tracked the seasons by the weather and the time of day by the sun or moon.

"Fucking winter will be here before you know it."

It had been a long time since he'd had any reason to keep up with time and the passage of time. Not since Kathy. When she was gone, nothing else mattered, not the day of the week or the month of the year. It was all useless now.

He, his wife, and their two children had lived in Timber Lake, South Dakota, a small town of less than six hundred people. He'd gone to work in the Saskatchewan territory of Canada for three weeks to a logging camp and come home to chaos and death a month later. Abe worked with a local logging company that had won a contract to harvest some prime timber not far over the border into Canada. He was only supposed to be gone twenty days, but when the disasters struck, getting back home had taken nearly an additional week.

At first, they hadn't really realized anything was wrong, but after riding out a couple of earthquakes and then not being able to get anyone on the radios or satellite phones, they decided the best thing was to head to Moose Jaw and find out what was going on. What they found had been almost surreal. In less than two weeks, the small city had fallen to marshal law with looting, raiding, and widespread panic. Already disease had gotten a foothold in some areas.

They headed back to the States with one thing on their mind, getting home to their families. The journey had taken longer with the continued quakes and flooded roads. Forest fires had broken out in some areas and one detour led to another until making it back home seemed almost impossible. Then once they drove into town, there wasn't much left of the place to call home.

Major floods, tornadoes, earthquakes, tsunamis, and diseases had wiped out most of the world's population. Disease tore through the country, targeting women, children, and the elderly. Abe pretty much ran the final miles to his place only to find the bodies of his wife and two children among the rubble that had once been their dream house.

Abe adjusted the fishing gear as he got a better grip on the basket holding his catch. The hike back to the lodge seemed to take twice as long today for some reason. It probably seemed that way because he couldn't stop remembering. Sometimes the memories would haunt him for days and sometimes he'd have to struggle to remember her face, the scent of her skin just after they'd made love.

He shook his head and trudged on. The garden wouldn't harvest itself, and the animals needed feeding. He didn't have time to waste thinking about what was gone. It was set in stone and would be there the next time he let his guard down and allowed the past to creep up on him.

When he stepped out of the tree line where he could see the structures that made up his home there in the Border Lands, Abe felt some of the tension of the last few minutes fall away. This was where he lived now, somewhere in the northwest part of what used to be Montana, near Yellowstone. His house was the lodge of what he had finally determined had once been a militia stronghold.

Besides all of the propaganda he found in the lodge and six cabins nestled in the forest around him, he'd also found hidden caches of guns, ammunition, and supplies all over the area. The place hadn't been totally abandoned, though. Abe had to bury several bodies before he could claim the place as his.

He checked his trip wires to be sure no one had been there before stepping inside the large building. Stowing the fishing gear, the next thing on his list was to finish cleaning the fish and cooking them up. An early lunch would be welcome after the morning he'd had. Then it was back outside to work in the garden and feed the animals.

Looking out the window toward the barn, the emptiness that filled him seemed greater for some reason. Maybe it would continue to grow until it ate him alive, leaving nothing behind but a shell. Then maybe he could lie down and not get back up.

* * * *

Russell Coggins walked right into the damn thing. He'd been so wrapped up in self-pity that he'd completely missed hearing a massive grizzly bear rooting around ahead of him. When he almost bounced off the bastard, it stood on its hind legs and roared at him. It had to be nearly eight feet tall with claws like razor blades.

"Aw, hell! Son of a bitch!"

Russell struggled to keep his balance while tearing away from the hold the bear had on his shoulder and backpack. He could feel the slightly curved claws tearing into him. If he fell, he would be dead for sure. As it was, he'd be lucky to get away without losing his fucking arm.

"Let go, you fucking bastard." He managed to free his knife and jab the grizzly in the gut.

The animal's deafening roar left his ears ringing, but he was free to scramble for safety. There was no way he could climb a tree with his injured shoulder. He veered away from them and aimed for the rocks ahead. If he could make it to them, he would have a chance of maneuvering through them, where the much bigger bear wouldn't be able to follow.

The blood dripping from his shoulder and arm made negotiating the massive stones difficult. Added to that, one of the straps on the backpack was torn apart so that he had to carry it. He managed to climb up a short ways then slip between the rock outcropping where the angry predator couldn't reach him. Now all he had to do was manage to stop the bleeding and dress the wounds. Hopefully they wouldn't need stitches. Russell wasn't counting on his luck holding out for that, though.

Most of his wounds were on the back part of his shoulder, so he couldn't reach them or even see them to figure out how bad they were. He pulled out a folded shirt and shifted it between him and the rock he was leaning against, pressing back to apply pressure to the area while he tended to the areas he could reach.

Pain began to beat out the endorphins that had briefly masked it, making concentrating arduous. Slowly he worked through the pain until dizziness proved focusing to be impossible. Though he could no longer see the grizzly, he could still hear him on the other side of the rocks. It didn't seem to have anywhere pressing to go at the moment, which left him in dire straits. Without medical attention soon, he'd either bleed to death or end up with a massive infection that he had no way of treating. Not to mention that he didn't have enough food or water for more than one day. Even if he managed to hold the rifle up, he wouldn't be able to aim it and would only piss the grizzly off more if he somehow managed to hit it.

"Hell, even if I could get out of here, I'm in no shape to hunt or get water." He was dead.

He held out no hope that anyone would come to his rescue. There had been no sign of anyone in the last three days he'd been walking and before that, he hadn't seen anyone in nearly a week.

"Face it, Russ. This is it for you. If you're lucky, the good Lord will have mercy and take you in to be with Jill and the girls." He chuckled weakly.

He didn't hold out much hope of that. Why hadn't he died back with Jill during the raid instead of months later, out here all alone? It didn't make sense. At least his son was safe. He'd been smart not to come with him. Moving in with Peggy and her husband to form a ménage had been a good idea after all. Russell hadn't liked the idea at first, but after losing Jill to the damn black-market traders, he could see the wisdom in it now. Two or even three men could protect a woman much better than just one.

"I miss you so damn much, Jill. I'm sorry I was too possessive and jealous to allow another man to help me keep you safe. I was a fool." He sighed.

He was so tired that he couldn't hold back the silent tears that leaked from his eyes. She had been his high-school sweetheart. They'd married right after graduation. He went to work on the barges that ran up and down the rivers, making good money while she worked part-time at a department store in town and took care of the house and eventually their three children.

He could almost see her waiting on him when he would get off the boat after working thirty days in a row. He'd have the next two weeks off to make it up to her. They'd had a good life, with the normal ups and downs. Then hell opened up and all but swallowed the world in one gulp.

He would never forget the earthquakes and how they'd screwed up the currents in the river. They'd lost two men off the barge and couldn't find them. Then the rain had trapped them for nearly a week because of all the debris in the river. The morning the captain hadn't been able to raise anyone on the radio he'd had a bad feeling, but they continued on. The cell phones didn't work either, making the men edgy and short tempered.

When they had finally made it back to port, it was to find chaos everywhere. Storms that had dumped massive amounts of rain on the already earthquake-torn earth had also spawned killer tornadoes. Russell managed to make it back to the neighborhood where he and his family lived outside of St. Louis, Missouri, but once there, he'd had to walk and search for his home. The devastation was immense, mind-boggling in its magnitude.

Fragmented memories of finding Jill and his son living in a tent near the ruin of their home plagued him as he tried to ignore how his teeth were chattering. He knew it was the beginnings of shock.

She and their son had buried their two daughters while he'd been gone. He could still hear her anguish as she told him about their deaths. The three of them had mourned over their graves together then he had picked up what was left of his family and joined others to find shelter and food.

After nearly two years of barely surviving the continued devastation and diseases, the city grew too dangerous with gangs and black-market traders. They gathered everything they could scrounge and joined a caravan of survivors heading for the Border Lands, where it was rumored living off the land was safer. It took them over a week to locate a small community of people who had settled in houses that had been abandoned or where the occupants had died.

For the next five years, they led a relatively happy existence. It hadn't been easy by any means, but until the black-market traders had shown up, life had been livable. But nothing lasts forever. He'd learned that lesson. Despite being urged by others to bring in another man to help keep his wife safe, Russell had balked at sharing his wife. It wasn't right. Besides, he could keep her safe. He didn't need help taking care of his woman.

"Stupid, stupid, stupid," he muttered to himself.

It was getting to be midafternoon now, and his shoulder was mostly numb. He hoped he would go to sleep soon and the cold would finish him as he rested.

"Coward. Jill would call you a coward for giving up, Russ."

She had been hanging out clothes in the unseasonably warm spring air when the men had attacked. Their son wasn't there. He'd been talking to another family about moving in with them to be their third. He and his son had argued over that frequently, but now he was glad his son hadn't been there, or he might have died, too.

He heard her scream from the barn and grabbed his rifle as he took off toward the house. The clothes basket was upturned and the basket of clips emptied on the ground beneath the clothesline. He remembered storming into the house to find his sweet Jillian fighting the two men attempting to tie her up. A red haze had covered his eyes, and he lifted his rifle to shoot one of the men. Only there had been three of them, not two. The third man had been searching the upstairs and managed to get off a shot as he raced down the staircase. The sting of the bullet hitting his shoulder hadn't really registered at first, but it had thrown his aim off and he only winged one of the men holding Jill.

The distraction gave her the opportunity to slip through them and run. She headed for the front door and managed to get outside. He managed to shoot the man on the stairs before he got off another shot but had to chase after the other two traders as they followed his wife. Russell was scared to shoot for fear of hitting Jill.

Just as they reached the barn, a shot whizzed past his head, missing the two men in front of him and struck Jill in the chest. Seeing her fall to the ground had broken something inside of him. He roared out in denial before turning and shooting the bastard behind him in the head. Then he killed the other two men after cornering them in the barn. Afterwards he'd wished he hadn't killed them so quickly. They hadn't deserved such a quick end.

After he had recovered enough to travel, Russell had said good-bye to his son and the people he'd called friends for so many years. Without Jill, he was like a ship without an anchor. He needed to go.

It dawned on him that the damn bear had moved on. He couldn't hear it anymore. Not that it really mattered now anyway. He didn't have the energy to go anywhere. Still, he should at least make an effort to flag where he was in case someone did happen along. Maybe they would find his body and give it a proper burial instead of leaving him for the scavengers.

Even though he was weak from blood loss and stiff from passing so many hours in one position, Russell managed to shove the empty backpack through the crevice he'd squeezed through to escape the bear.

The last thing he thought about as he closed his eyes was to hope the fucking bear hurt as badly as he did.

Chapter Two

"Damn deer. They were here earlier."

Abe stood up from where he'd been crouched, waiting for the mule deer to return along the path they had been using the last few days. Why had they changed their pattern?

Stretching to relieve his cramped muscles, exasperation had him muttering curses under his breath. Nothing had gone right the over the last week. The fucking tractor had broken down before he'd finished tilling up the garden for the winter, and he'd had to reshoe his horse. Then there'd been the fence down that had taken all of a day to repair.

"I'm going to kill a damn deer today if it's the last fucking thing I do."

He grabbed his light pack and eased through the woods in search of something to shoot at. Right about then, he would have been happy with killing Bugs Bunny.

The smell of blood hit him first. No wonder the deer hadn't followed their normal trail. Something was dying or dead close by. He tried to pinpoint the direction of the wind to determine which way to go. Finally he chose north and walked with his rifle at the ready. The ground began to change to a slight incline as the trees began to thin. A muted grunt had him stopping in his tracks. He looked around before noticing a massive lump on the ground ahead of him in the shadows.

The lump made a noise again that sounded like raspy breathing. Abe slowly moved toward it. When he was within fifteen feet, he could tell it was a grizzly. It wasn't the smartest thing he'd ever done and could easily be the dumbest if he lived to tell about it, but Abe picked his way closer to the beast. He could easily hear gurgling now.

Whatever had happened to it, a lung was involved. Something had managed to do enough damage that it was bleeding into its lungs.

Taking another step closer, he nudged it with the barrel of the rifle, ready to shoot if the bear moved. It didn't. The bubbly noises grew fainter. It was dying. He wondered what had gotten the best of the massive grizzly. Short of man, they didn't have a lot of natural predators.

Abe walked around it and followed its path to see if he would find another dead or dying animal wherever the original fight had taken place. Instead, he found more blood and a trail that led toward a cropping of rocks. Cougar maybe? They would have gone to higher ground if injured.

As he eased closer to the area, something that didn't belong grabbed his attention. A cloth bag of some kind was stuck between two boulders. When he was able to see it better, he found it was what was left of a backpack and was covered in blood. That didn't bode well for whoever had been carrying it. The blood trail let straight to the rocks, but other than the smears all over the bottom boulders, he didn't see any additional blood on the rocks above to suggest that they had managed to climb to safety.

He crouched down and pulled the bag out of the crevice, exposing a bloodied hand that had probably been gripping it. Peering deeper into the opening, Abe could barely make out the shape of a man.

"Fuck!" He reached in and touched his fingers to the man's wrist to check for a pulse.

Fully expecting not to find one, the weak flutter startled him into action. The crevice widened at the top, allowing him to crawl up and into the opening so that he could reach the stranger. It was a tight fit, but he managed to rearrange the man so that he could check where he was hurt. With the sun going down, seeing became an issue. The best he could tell, there were four deep furrows down the man's back and over his right shoulder as well as cuts on his arm and the upper portion of his chest. It looked as if he'd lost a lot of blood as well.

Thankfully, the wounds were no longer actively bleeding. He was afraid that once he started moving him, that would change.

Abe climbed back out and gathered just the supplies he'd need from his pack and returned to dress the worst of the wounds. Then he hoisted the unconscious man up and onto the top of one of the massive rocks. After shoving what was left of his supplies and the stranger's rifle through the opening, he climbed out and carefully lowered the man off the rock. He had no choice but to carry him back to the lodge over his shoulder.

By the time he made it home, he was all but staggering from the added weight of the big man along with his own pack. He didn't bother checking his safety measures before stumbling into the building. Abe carried the man to the couch in front of the massive stone fireplace and sank to the floor on his knees. It took several minutes for him to catch his breath and manage to stand again. If the stranger was going to make it, he had to hurry.

Thanks to the previous owners, there were plenty of first aid supplies to choose from. After starting a fire in the fireplace to warm the large room, Abe gathered what he needed and got to work.

"Don't know why the hell I'm bothering. He's not going to make it anyway. He's lost too much blood."

Two hours later, the man still breathed, and Abe was taping the last section of bandage. It had taken an untold number of stitches to close the wounds that he felt comfortable sewing shut. The others he'd left to drain and close as they healed. It wouldn't do to close infection up to fester. It was a miracle the lucky bastard was still alive.

Without antibiotics to prevent infection, Abe was reduced to mixing up some herbal remedies he'd learned from some of the books he had found there at the compound. He managed to force some of one of the liquids down the man's throat and applied a poultice to the open wounds. All he could do now was watch and keep his patient warm and dry. If he got a fever, he'd try to cool him down, but there wasn't much more he could do.

"Guess time will tell if you live or die." He shook his head and walked away to take a shower and change clothes.

After ridding himself of the stench of blood and sweat, Abe raced through his chores and settled for a meal of dried meat and fruit before settling down to watch over the injured stranger. Normally he slept upstairs in one of the rooms, but with his patient on the couch in front of the fire, he decided he better stay close by. He covered up with a blanket and reclined in one of the lounge chairs for the night.

Every few hours, he got up and forced water and more of the homemade medicine down the man's throat. Around two in the morning, the stranger's fever went up enough that he was mumbling incoherently and thrashing about on the couch. Abe spent the next two hours bathing him in cool water and keeping him from further injuring himself.

All during the night and early morning, the deathly ill man mumbled and called out over and over about someone named Jill as well as the names Sandy, Will, and Janice. Abe figured it was the names of his family members who were more than likely dead. It reminded him of his own losses, triggering his anger.

"Fucking bastard will drive me crazy taking care of him, and then he'll die anyway. Don't know why I'm wasting time on him."

* * * *

Russell felt as if he were being burned alive. Pain tore through him with each rise and fall of his chest. So this was hell. He should have known there was no way God would have allowed him into heaven to be with his family, considering he hadn't been able to protect them to begin with. Eternal pain and that unending fire licking at his skin like a hungry lover would be his punishment.

No matter how hard he tried, he couldn't seem to escape either one as he tried to find a more comfortable position. It dawned on him that he couldn't see anything because his eyes were still closed. When he attempted to open them, they wouldn't budge. Where they sealed shut? Would endless blackness be part of this horrific torture?

Time passed as he floated in agony, but he had no idea how much. His only companion was pain and more pain. Slowly, the heat seemed to change. Suddenly, the searing sensations that had bubbled along his skin flipped to those of a burning cold that would surely freeze him to solid ice. He'd never heard of hell being cold, but then that old saying *when hell freezes over* seemed appropriate now. Maybe it had.

To add further misery to his abused existence, it felt as if someone was bathing him in icy water. He fought the invisible ministrations in hopes he could make it go away, but after a while, he stopped fighting. He was too tired and soul weary. Let the little demons do whatever they wanted to him. He'd give them no further pleasure fighting them.

After a while, he drifted some more, and Russell realized that he no longer seemed to hurt as badly and the devastating heat and breath-stealing cold had disappeared. Was this a new kind of torture? Would he float there, always wondering what would happen next, waiting for the next round of torment to start?

Take the reprieve for what it is, Russell. I don't need to bring more pain on myself by trying to anticipate the next round of assault.

For what seemed like forever, Russell floated in a sea of nothingness with occasional bouts of fire that blistered his skin and cold that burned his lungs. Sometimes he felt as if someone was torturing him, but most of the time, he felt completely and utterly alone. Not even thoughts of his family seemed to penetrate his existence at those times. True despondency settled over him like a skin-tight leather suit. It filled every nook and cranny, leaving behind no room for hope of any kind.

Out of nowhere, something jerked his eyes open to a blinding bright light. His eyes watered at the suddenness of it. Without thinking, he tried to cover his eyes with his hand and yelled out at the intense pain that caused. His right arm and shoulder felt as if he'd ripped it off his body.

"What in the hell are you trying to do? If you bust those stitches open, I'll kill you."

Russell snapped his eyes to the left and the image of a huge bear of a man stared back at him from less than four feet away. Confusion clogged his head with splintered memories of what had happened to him. All he could remember was burying his sweet Jill and traveling on foot to get away from the pain. From the feel of it, he'd only managed to find more pain. What the hell?

"Who are you?" he finally asked.

"Abraham Waverly. Call me Abe." His voice was gruff and deep.

Russell just closed his eyes for what he thought had only been a second, but when he opened them again, the man was gone. He took advantage of being along again and studied the room around him. From what he could tell from his position on the couch that felt like good leather, he was in a rather large room that had a massive stone fireplace and hearth. The mantel was a large, rough-hewn slice of wood.

There were built-in shelves on each side of the stone chimney that stretched to the top of the vaulted ceiling. They were filled with books. He couldn't see anything more than what was in front of him from his limited vantage point. The room felt massive around him. Judging from the height of the ceiling, it was huge.

"I see you're finally awake again." The stranger appeared next to the couch. He picked something up and walked closer, where he knelt down in front of the couch and held a cup to Russell's lips. "Try to drink some water. If you can take this and keep it down, I'll give you some broth later."

His seemingly reluctant host stood up again and walked out of his range of sight. He kept waiting for him to return, but after several minutes, Russell gave up and closed his eyes again. The water had been a blessing. Maybe the stranger would return soon with the promised broth. He was hungry.

He spent another long while of floating, thinking over the new turn of events at finding that he wasn't dead and suffering in hell after all. Who was the man who was grudgingly helping him? No doubt he had his own sorrowful tale. No one who lived through the horrific year of catastrophes was without sorrow and loss. No doubt Russell's presence was an irritant to the big man.

He figured Abe to be about six and a half feet tall and weigh a good two hundred seventy pounds. He was solidly built without an ounce of fat on him, from what little he had seen of the man. His shaggy black hair and bushy dark beard covered his face, but dark piercing eyes sealed his perception of the man as being unsociable, even unapproachable in his demeanor. Why had the man bothered with trying to save him in the first place? It had to have been a long shot at best. Hell, he could still die of pneumonia or a wound infection.

The sound of boots scraping across the floor pulled him back from his musings. He opened his eyes again. Abe walked into view with a bowl in his hands. He set it on the table by the couch then disappeared for a second before returning with a straight chair in tow. He plopped it down in front of Russell, and after retrieving the bowl from the table, sat down and stared at him.

"Hope you're hungry. I'm not a great cook, but it's edible and filling." He stirred the contents of the bowl before spooning up some and offering it to him.

Russell struggled to drink it while lying flat on his back. Some of it dribbled out of his mouth.

"Fuck. I need to sit you up some. Hold on." He got up and set the bowl back on the table with a sigh.

The next thing Russell knew, the big man had pulled him up on the couch like he weighed nothing. For a few seconds, he couldn't think, much less curse due to the pain that robbed his ability to draw a complete breath. When it finally eased some, he gasped for breath and glared at the other man now sitting back in the chair with the bowl in his hands.

"Hell, fire, and damnation! Did you have to be so rough?"

Abe frowned before speaking. "Uh, sorry. Guess I wasn't thinking past getting you up so you could eat."

He pushed the spoon of broth at his mouth. Russell continued to scowl at the man as he opened his mouth and swallowed the broth. After a few seconds of silence as the man fed him, Russell realized that while a little bland, the broth was pretty damn good, but then again, he hadn't had anything to eat in a while, either. He wondered how long it had been since he and the bear had met up.

"How long have I been here?"

"'Bout three days. Surprised the hell out of me that you lived." Abe spooned the last of the liquid from the bowl into Russell's mouth.

"Uh, thanks for helping me." Russell looked down at his hand. His other arm was pretty much bandaged to his chest.

"Not out of the woods yet." Abe got up and took both the chair and the bowl with him when he walked off.

Russell sighed. The other man didn't seem to have much to say, and he was chock-full of positive thoughts. Not that it hadn't been what he had been thinking earlier anyway. It just seemed a little harsh coming from someone else.

A few minutes later, Abe returned to the living room and added a log to the fire. He turned around and leaned against the mantel with one arm. He just stared at Russell for a few seconds as if trying to make up his mind about something. Finally he let out a deep breath and spoke up.

"You'd probably like to know that you managed to get a killing blow in on that bear you tangled with. Hit his lung. I found him a little ways into the woods, drawing his last breath."

"Well, hell. Figured all I did was piss him off more. Did you get anything good out of him before the scavengers got to him?"

Abe shrugged. "Didn't bother with the meat since by the time I made it back from sewing you up and tending to things around her, it had been too long. I did skin him though. Got his hide stretched out in the barn."

"Well, thanks again for bothering with me. You live here alone?" Russell figured he did, since he hadn't seen anyone else around when he'd been lucid.

"Yep. Not many folks venture this deep in the woods or this far north. Like it fine like that, too."

"I understand. That's why I headed this way, myself. I'll be out of your hair as soon as I get back on my feet."

"So long as you don't make a nuisance of yourself, there's no hurry. Besides, winter is about here. You won't make it without somewhere to hunker down." Abe's gruff words surprised him.

Before Russell could say anything, the big man stomped off. A few seconds later, a door behind him slammed shut. He guessed as far as welcomes went, he'd just gotten his.

Chapter Three

The wind grew colder with each step Celina Berry took, and the weight of the oversized backpack seemed to increase as well. She had no idea where she was or even if she was heading in the right direction. She glanced up at the darkening sky and prayed she would find shelter soon. She would never survive out in the open at night with the cold wind and dangerous animals roaming about.

She refused to break down and cry while she needed to concentrate on staying upright. When she found somewhere safe to rest, she would let her heart weep for all that she had lost. Celina continued to keep the river on her left in sight and followed it as close as she was able. It was the only constant landmark she could remember from the map. Too bad it had been covered in blood and made worthless.

Her mind wondered as she trudged on. Memories of she and Roger clinging to each other during that horrifying year where the world as she'd known it had ceased to exist, teased her mind. They'd been twenty and newlyweds, giddy with love and proud of their two-bedroom rental house in Knoxville, Tennessee. Then everything blew up on them. The killer storms with multiple tornadoes that left little behind. The rain had led to floods that led to disease. The earthquakes buried what the tornadoes had toppled. There had been so little left of the bustling city they'd both grown up in.

Celina had to take a detour around an area that was so overgrown with briars and bushes she couldn't force her way through it. She prayed that she would be able to make it back to the river once she got around the mess. With the wind howling through the treetops, the normally loud river seemed muted and a long ways off.

Her pack got caught on a branch as she forced her way through yet another group of waist-high bushes. She had to slip her arms out of the pack in order to work it free of the stubborn branch holding it hostage. Finally, with the pack firmly back in place, Celina continued forging her way through the dense, drying vegetation. She nearly fell over when she pushed through a particularly stubborn area to step into a fairly open area in front of an old cabin.

Relief flooded her as she walked closer to the building. It wasn't in great shape, but it would certainly do as shelter for the night. She pulled her husband's rifle off her shoulder and wrapped the strap around her hand like he'd shown her how to do before inching her way inside the doorway.

With barely enough light to see the inside of the cabin through the still-intact dirty windows, Celina watched around her for anything that moved as she stepped deeper into the large room. There wasn't much in the way of furnishings. A double bed in one corner looked as if it had seen better days. A loveseat and moldy chair took up an area in front of the fireplace and a small kitchen table with two chairs sat off to the side in front of a sink, stove, and refrigerator.

Everything looked too dirty to actually use, but the roof seemed to be intact, so it would offer shelter from the wind and rain, if it were to fall. She set the heavy pack on the hearth and shoved the warped door of the cabin as closed as it would go. As much as she would have liked to have built a fire in the fireplace, she had no idea if it would be safe or not. The chimney wouldn't have been cleaned out for at least the last seven years, she was pretty sure.

Celina spent the next hour cleaning off a place in front of the hearth and making a bed. She found musty but clean linens in a closet in the bathroom to act as the buffer between her and the drafty floor. After making do with a meal of cold beans and some jerky, she snuggled down, wearing all of her clothes and covered with a blanket from her pack. The pack itself made an uncomfortable pillow, but she could make do. It was all she knew how to do now.

When she slept, the dreams came. They always started off with her and her husband, Roger, living in their apartment, secure in their little world. Then they drifted forward to after the disasters to when they had found friends in a small community deep in the Border Lands. They had lived there for nearly six years in relative peace before things started to fall apart again.

First had been the poor crops that had seriously depleted everyone's supplies. The wolves had always been a problem, but then they started attacking people out in the open in broad daylight. They had lost all fear of man, even with their guns. When the black-market traders and agents started stealing women, everyone had begun to panic. Families moved in with each other for safety.

Celina knew what was coming as the dream continued, but she was powerless to stop it. They hadn't moved closer to the others yet. Roger wanted to wait until after they had finished harvesting the last of their garden to make the move. She had been scared of waiting, and they'd fought each night about it. They would only lose a few tomatoes, peppers, and some late-maturing beans. It hadn't been worth it when it was all said and done.

They woke to smoke filling the bedroom. She immediately knew it was the black-market agents since they were known for burning families out of their homes to kidnap the women and any female children they could find. Roger had grabbed his gun and pulled out the packs from beneath the bed that they kept filled and ready, should they need them.

She followed Roger as she held a cloth over her mouth. They managed to get downstairs and into the hall bathroom. They had started the fire on the outside in front of the house. It meant the only way out should have been through the kitchen door. They would be waiting on them there. Roger had reworked the bathroom window there so that they could climb through it. Now if only they would be lucky enough that none of their attackers saw them escape.

In her dream, everything went well. Roger hadn't been shot as they slipped into the woods. They had made it to the edge of their neighbor's property to find Bess and her husband, Claude, at home, along with another family that had moved in with them. They managed to kill the agents and all seemed well.

As it normally did, her dream turned to a nightmare, and Celina woke screaming for Roger. Clutching her belly as the memory of struggling to bury him pulled sobs from deep inside, she promised the unborn child she carried that she would protect it with her life.

* * * *

The next morning, the sun was once again shining as she pulled the backpack on and pulled the door open. The temperature outside wasn't as chilly as she had expected after such a cold wind the night before. She walked to the edge of the clearing and listened for the sound of the river. After nearly a full minute of standing absolutely still, she couldn't hear it. What was she going to do now? Without the river as her landmark, Celina had no idea which way to go.

She had roughly enough food, if she was stingy, to last another full day. After that, she would go hungry. Should she stay where she was and hope someone would come along, or should she continue in hopes she would stumble across another home that included canned food?

Tears pricked at the back of her eyes. Refusing to give in to them, Celina chose a direction, using the sun, and stepped into the forest. Small rodents scampered ahead of her as she forced herself to put one foot in front of the other. At times there were birds flitting from branch to branch above her head and other times the woods around her was quiet except for the sound of her breathing and noisy movements through dry leaves and branches.

Twice she stopped to rest, and each time it became harder and harder to make herself continue. When she broke through the trees into an open area where rocks and small boulders lay at the base of a large hill, she felt like giving up. It was midafternoon by the level of the sun, and she had no idea if she was near anywhere that would provide shelter or not. Her legs tingled with exhaustion, and she was covered in scratches from the briars and low-hanging branches.

She walked over to the rocks and climbed up until she found one flat enough she could curl up and take a nap. She prayed she would be safe enough up off the ground like she was. Maybe once she had rested for an hour she would be able to continue. As it stood now, Celina didn't have the energy to take even one more step. Using the backpack as a body pillow of sorts, she curled around it and settled on the sun-warmed rock and fell asleep.

* * * *

Russell followed Abe as they walked through the woods. The other man was showing him around the area so he wouldn't get lost if he went walking by himself. This was only the third day he'd been outside since his attack by the bear. It had been over two weeks, and he had been getting restless. Abe was taking him on short walks twice a day to build up his strength and familiarize him with everything.

They hadn't discussed him moving on again since Abe had made the comment that with winter around the corner, he might as well stay there. Russell found that he liked the man despite his snarly attitude and antisocial behavior. He could relate in a way. He didn't much feel like talking, either. What was there to talk about anyway?

"We'll stop up ahead where there's a giant rock pile. We'll rest there for a few minutes," Abe said.

Russell just shook his head. The big man meant so *Russell* could rest. Abe didn't need to rest. He could probably walk all day without stopping. The guy was a mountain of a man with strength that blew him away. Russell was no midget at six feet, two inches, but he had nothing on Abe.

"Can't stay long," Abe said as they stepped out of the trees. "Need to get back and chop some more wood. Going to snow tomorrow night or the next day."

"How do you know that?" Russell looked up and didn't see a cloud in the sky.

The other man didn't answer him and had stopped dead still in the middle of the clearing. Russell nearly ran into the back of him. Sensing that something was wrong, he didn't move either, in case there was a wild animal on the rocks ahead. Standing where he was, Russell couldn't see around the other man to know what had spooked him.

"What is it?" he whispered.

"Not sure. Stay here." Abe's deep voice sounded rough in a whisper.

Russell watched as the other man walked straight ahead in slow measured steps. He swallowed, worried that at any minute, something would jump at his new friend. When nothing happened and Abe stopped less than a yard from the first set of rocks, Russell began to grow curious. He eased closer.

"Fuck. What is going on? When did it turn into Grand Central Station out here?" Disgust was evident in the other man's voice.

Just as Russell made it even with the other man, a woman sat up from where she'd been lying on a rock slightly above them. Her wide, fawn-colored eyes took them both in with obvious nervousness.

"Are you okay?" Russell moved a few steps closer.

Abe turned and frowned at him. "Don't go talking to her, or she'll want to go back with us."

"Who are you?" Her soft, husky voice sent chills down his spine.

"I'm Russell, and this sociable guy is Abraham or Abe for short."

"Do you live near here?" She still didn't move, holding the backpack that looked bigger than she was in her lap.

"Not far from here. Where are you from?" Russell wondered why she was all alone out here in the woods.

"I'm originally from Tennessee. What about you?"

"Missouri." Russell nudged Abe in the arm.

"What?" He continued to stare at the woman.

"What's your name, ma'am?" Russell thought her golden-brown hair with its red highlights was beautiful even though it was a tangled mess.

"Celina. I'm looking for a safe place to live. Are there any empty homes near yours?"

"No."

"Yes."

Both Abe and Russell answered her question at the same time. They both glared at each other. It was obvious that Abe didn't want her around. Why was he being so hostile toward her? She was obviously in need of help. There was no way he could leave her there with night approaching.

"Abe! What is your problem?"

"I–I don't want to cause any trouble. I just want somewhere to spend the night. I'll keep going in the morning." She hugged the backpack tighter to her body.

"Why don't you let us help you down from there? It's going to get dark before long, so we need to get moving." Russell stepped closer to the rocks.

Abe let out a disgusted sigh and pushed Russell to the side. "You can't lift her until your shoulder heals up. I'll get her down."

Russell smothered a smile and waited to see what Celina would do. She hesitated for a second then held her pack out to the big man. He adjusted the straps then slipped it over his arms and settled it on his back before holding out his arms once again. She scooted closer to the edge of the rock and leaned forward with her arms outstretched so that Abe could scoop her off the rock. When he swung her off and stood her on her feet, Russell thought she was the cutest thing he'd ever seen.

"Better get going." Abe turned and led the way back toward the lodge.

Russell nodded for her to go next and he brought up the rear. It just seemed natural to put her in the middle where she would be the safest. Besides, he liked watching her as he walked. Her bulky coat hid her figure, but it didn't stop him from imagining what she would look like once the coat came off. Then a picture of his late wife flashed in his mind, and he instantly felt ashamed that he was ogling another woman. It didn't matter that it had been over fifteen months since he'd lost her. She had been his everything.

Abe's long stride was eating up the distance to the lodge and slowly putting space between them. He sighed and called out to get him to slow down. After that, the other man would turn to check their progress every few minutes. Why had the man been so short with Celina? It wasn't her fault she was lost and alone in the woods.

When they reached the edge of the clearing that surrounded the lodge and its outbuildings, Russell felt relief flow over him. His shoulder was aching some, and it was obvious that Celina was about at the end of her endurance. To her credit, she hadn't complained once about Abe's pace. He doubted she would have said a word even if he'd walked out of sight. She struck him as stubborn by the lift of her chin when she'd spoken to them earlier.

Abe reached the lodge door and opened it. He left it open for them to enter behind him but had already reached the fireplace and was adding a log when Russell closed and locked the door behind them. While the other man tended to the fire, he began to pull off his outerwear and hang it on one of the many hooks on the wall by the door.

"Take off your coat and go over to the fireplace so you can get warm," Russell suggested.

She dipped her head and unzipped the coat, shrugging out of it as she did. He was busy removing his boots when the sound of a log hitting the floor jerked his eyes toward Abe. The other man was staring at Celina as she stretched to hang up her coat. Russell frowned. What was Abe's deal? He was just about to ask the other man when she turned around and he noticed the slightly rounded mound of Celina's abdomen where her shirt was stretched tightly over it. Celina was pregnant.

Chapter Four

"You're pregnant," Russell spit out.

"Um, yeah. Somewhere around four months, I think."

She didn't seem to notice that they were both staring at her stomach. Abe bent to pick up the log he'd dropped and focused his attention on seeing about the fire. The sight of her slightly rounded belly had shocked him. He couldn't remember the last time he'd seen a woman, much less a pregnant one. What in the hell was she doing out there all alone? Fuck! What were they going to do with her?

"What are you doing way out here all alone, Celina?" Russell asked.

Abe pretended to be busy with the fire as he listened to them talk. His heart was thumping along like a freight train. He was afraid that if he stopped to look at his hands he'd find them shaking.

"My husband and I were trying to find somewhere safer to live. Black-market agents burned us out of our last home, and Roger was injured when we ran. He died a few weeks back."

Abe winced at the obvious pain in the woman's voice. He knew that feeling well. With a tired sigh, he returned the poker to the stand and turned from the fire to watch them. Celina had taken a seat on the couch in front of him with Russell sitting on the edge of one of the chairs. He moved over some so as not to block the heat from the fire.

"I'm sorry for your loss. I guess we all know about loss. Still, carrying a child and all is going to be hard for you. Where were you heading?" Russell was absently rubbing his injured shoulder.

"Thanks." She drew in a deep breath. Tears glistened in her eyes. "I don't know where to go. I was just trying to keep moving until I found somewhere I could stay."

"There are several cabins around the lodge here. I'm sure one of them would be in good enough shape for you to live in over the winter." Abe felt Russell's eyes on him like a hot iron.

"No!"

No doubt Russell expected him to agree and offer her the place. Before Abe knew what he was going to say, he was offering her a room in the lodge.

"You don't need to be out there alone. Anything could happen. There are plenty of empty rooms here in the lodge. You can pick whichever one you want and we'll get it cleaned up." He stepped away from the fire. "I'm going to see about making something to eat. Russell, take her upstairs so she can pick out a room."

With that, he pushed through the door into the kitchen and breathed a sigh of relief to be out of her presence. His pulse refused to settle down despite the fact he'd put distance between them. He couldn't figure out why she affected him this way. She really wasn't anything special to look at. Well, except for those amazing honey-brown eyes and all that golden-brown hair. It was a rat's nest right now, but he was sure it would look glorious when it was clean and brushed until it was shiny and soft.

Disgusted with where his thoughts were headed, Abe concentrated on what to make to eat. He was sure she would be hungry, and it had been a long time since lunch for him and Russell. He stomped around, gathering what he needed and mumbled to himself as he prepared the meal. He couldn't help but wonder what they were doing in the other room or if they had gone upstairs to check out the empty rooms. Something inside of him needed to know where she was. He snorted with displeasure that he couldn't seem to put her out of his mind for long.

Once dinner was ready, Abe shoved the kitchen door open wide and started to call out to them to come eat while it was hot, but they weren't in the living room. He walked over to the stairs and bellowed up to the second floor.

"Dinner's ready. Get down here and eat while it's hot." He didn't wait around to listen for an answer.

When they walked through the kitchen door five minutes later, Abe was already eating at the table. He knew it was rude of him, but he didn't need to encourage Celina to get attached to him. He wasn't someone she should want to depend on. Abe was a loner and liked it that way. Up until Russell had shown up and now her, he hadn't seen anyone in a long time and those times had been from afar. Suddenly now, he had two people staying in his lodge. It was enough to give him a complex.

"This is good, Abe. Thanks for making it," Celina said in that low, husky voice of hers.

He grunted and continued eating.

"She picked the room next to yours because it has a bathroom connected to it." Russell finally spoke up after a few minutes of silence. "The bathroom will need some cleaning, but the bedroom was actually in good shape. We went ahead and changed the sheets to fresh ones."

"Good." He should have known she would choose that room. "There's plenty more to eat on the stove. Help yourself."

When he risked a glance up, it was to find her staring at him with a puzzled expression across her cute face.

"What?"

"If you don't want me here…"

"I didn't say that, did I?" He glowered and continued eating.

"Don't mind him. He's gruff and growls a lot, but he's pretty harmless."

Abe's frown deepened. He didn't know about harmless. Still, she had nothing to fear from him. Out of nowhere, worry for her condition blindsided him. How was she going to be able to cope with a baby to care for? What would happen when it came time for the baby's birth? She would be all alone somewhere and probably terrified.

This didn't sit well with him. He stood up and carried his plate to the sink. She would never survive on her own somewhere, and he knew for a fact that there was no one out this direction for miles and miles. He struggled to get everything done now, and sometimes it was damn near hand to mouth in having enough to eat. She would never be able to carve out a living without a man to help her. Not with a baby.

A feminine hand joined his in the sink, sliding her plate into the water. He turned to find her smiling shyly at him. Their eyes held for a few seconds until he tore his gaze away and concentrated on washing the dishes.

"I'll help. You cooked. You shouldn't have to do the dishes, too."

"I'm used to it. Didn't have anyone here with me 'til someone opened the gate and let the cows through."

Her warm laughter startled him. He jerked and stepped to the side. She was lovely when she laughed like that.

"Russell. I think he's calling us cows," she said.

"That's better than what he's called me in the past. Be flattered," the other man said.

Abe grunted and returned to washing the dishes. He wasn't sure what to make of the woman. Worse than that, he wasn't sure what to do with her either.

* * * *

Celina couldn't help but smile to herself at the crabby mountain of a man next to her. She dried the plates and carefully stacked them on the counter next to them. He acted like a bastard at times, but she saw glimpses of a kinder, gentler soul beneath all of the blunder. She couldn't help but wonder which was indicative of the true man.

"That's the last of it." Abe handed her a glass to dry. "I'll put them away. You don't know where they go, and in the lamplight, it would be hard to figure out."

She nodded and stepped back after drying off the glass. She watched as he quickly cleared the stack of clean dishes from the counter. The man was easily six and a half feet tall. His shaggy rich black hair brushed his shoulders and often formed a veil over his face. His dark beard covered the lower half of his face, making it difficult to tell his mood at times. It was just as bushy as his hair. She knew shaving could be a hassle for a man, and the heavy covering of hair probably shielded his face from the bitter cold of winter this far north.

She couldn't help but admire how easily he moved despite his massive size. Thinking of him as a mountain seemed appropriate. His broad shoulders topped a massively wide chest that, even covered by the shirt he wore, did little to subtract from the strength it contained. All of that muscular thickness tapered to a narrow waist before leading her eyes to somewhere she had no business thinking about. Regardless, she couldn't overlook the impressive bulge at the apex of his long, massive legs.

A shiver of awareness traveled down her spine. She immediately felt guilty. She'd just lost her husband who'd been the most important person in her life, and here she was ogling another man. Shame burned her face, and she turned away, her hand going to where her baby rested. She needed to get out of there and settle her mind. There was no future in where her mind was drifting.

"I'm going to go sit in front of the fire. Thanks again for dinner. It was very good." She quickly escaped, but not before she heard his typical grunt of acknowledgement.

Celina joined Russell in the living room, where the man stood with his back to the roaring fire. She curled her legs under her as she settled on the couch. The other man smiled but didn't say anything at first. His silence didn't bother her at first, but the longer it stretched, the more uncomfortable she grew. Finally, she spoke up.

"How long have you been here?"

"Only a couple of weeks. I had a run in with a grizzly, and Abe patched me up when he found me. I'm still not quite a hundred percent yet."

She nodded, studying the man. Russell looked to be closer to forty, though Abe seemed more experienced. Abe was probably a few years younger. Where Abe towered over both of them, Russell was still tall at a few inches over six feet. His shaggy auburn hair complemented his sky-blue eyes. Like Abe, he had a muscular body that came from long hours of hard work. She doubted either man held an ounce of fat anywhere on their bodies.

She tore her eyes from him just as they had settled on the inspiring package between his legs. When she leveled her gaze on his face, it was obvious that he knew where she'd been looking. Once again, heat warmed her cheeks. She quickly lowered her gaze to her hands.

"How did you end up way out here?" Russell asked, strolling over to the chair on her right.

Celina continued to look down at her hands as she relayed the events that had led to her being there all alone.

"Roger and I had been living just inside the Border Lands with some other families for several years. Then we started having trouble with black-market agents. They kept attacking us no matter what we did. Most of the families had doubled up, thinking there was strength in numbers."

She risked a glance over at the other man and found his gaze glued to the fire. His face held sadness and maybe a touch of guilt. She wasn't sure.

"My husband didn't want to live with others like that and balked at the thought of, um, sharing me with another man. After the second time the men tried to take me, he agreed that when we harvested the last of our garden, we'd move in with one of the others there. But the next day, they set fire to the house and we had to run for our lives. Roger was shot in the back, and eventually, the infection killed him."

"We believe that we don't need help keeping what we see as ours alone safe. It's a fool's folly in arrogance and conceit." Russell's voice held such torment that she knew he'd lost his wife under similar circumstances.

"And believing that any of us can defy fate is just as much an exercise in futility as capturing the sun or the moon." Abe walked farther into the room to stand by the hearth. "You're better off accepting what you have at the moment and avoid planning for it to be there the next day."

Celina thought that to be a very fatalistic and bitter way to live one's life, but didn't say as much out loud. Instead she changed the subject.

"The cabins you talked about, Russell, are they close to the main lodge?"

"Some are and some are deeper in the woods. Why?"

"I was thinking that maybe I could pick one to live in that was in fair enough shape and work on it when the weather permits."

Abe spoke up almost before she'd even finished her sentence. "No. I already told you that it's too dangerous for you to live alone in one of them. Has nothing in your past made an impression on you? You *can't* live alone, especially with a child. Think about your baby, if not yourself."

She cringed at the insinuation that she would intentionally place her child in harm's way. She would never do that, but what choice did she have? She was alone and had nowhere to go. At least she would be close to them if she needed them. Of course, that meant they would have to care enough to help her in the first place. Again she winced inwardly. They had already helped her. She couldn't fault them in her troubles.

"What are you thinking so hard about over there?" Russell's question reminded her that she wasn't alone.

"Just trying to figure out what I'm going to do. Abe's right. I have to think of my baby. I would never survive alone, much less with a helpless baby to care for."

"Stop fretting about it. You're safe enough here." Abe turned toward the fire and grabbed the poker from the stand. "It's winter now, and the snows will set in soon. You're not going anywhere before spring, so stop wasting your time worrying."

Celina stared at his back as he punched at the partially consumed logs, sending sparks floating up the chimney. She couldn't figure him out. One moment he acted like her staying there would be the worst torture a man could weather, and the next he was telling her she had no choice and to stop worrying over the future.

Fine, it was obvious that she had no real choice in the matter considering the time of year, but it didn't mean she was going to stand for his churlish attitude while she was there. A small smile escaped despite her best efforts to contain it. She would smother him with kindness and give him something to be irritated about. It would be her job to annoy him at every turn. He didn't know it yet, but she'd always taken great pride in being excellent in her work. Let the games begin.

She slowly stretched out her legs and stood up from the couch. Then she lifted her arms and stretched them as well. She was well aware of both men's appraisal when she did. Though it made her slightly uncomfortable, she really didn't feel that she had anything to worry about from them. They didn't strike her as the type to force themselves on a woman, especially a pregnant one.

"I think I'm going to go on up to bed. I'm quite tired. You never really sleep well out in the open or when you're running from something." Celina turned and walked across the room to the staircase.

"Wait." Russell got up as well and snagged one of the lamps. "You'll need this to get ready for bed. I'll come up with you. I'm tired as well."

She didn't say anything, just waited on him to join her at the bottom of the stairs. As they ascended the staircase, she glanced over at where Abe still stood gazing at the fire with his back to them. He looked so incredibly alone, standing there like that. She figured this was how he looked at night all of the years before they had crashed unexpectedly into his life. Surely deep down he felt as if things had changed for the better.

Her view disappeared as they stepped closer to the second floor. The air up there was considerably colder. A slight shiver ran over her body.

"We'd better get you under the covers before you catch a cold. You need warmer clothes here, too. I'm sure we can find something for you around here somewhere." Russell increased his pace, leaving her little choice except to almost jog next to him.

At her door he handed her the lamp. At her attempt to refuse it, he assured her that he had one in his room he could light.

"Thank you, Russell. Hope you sleep well." She turned and opened the door.

"You, too, Celina. See you in the morning."

She turned to close the door but only saw his retreating form as he made his way to his own room down and across the hall a short ways. When she closed the door and turned around she was hit with a moment of déjà vu at how closely the room resembled the one she and Roger had shared for years before the attack. Putting it down to the soft shadows around the room from the lamp, she brushed the sensation away and located the drawer she'd found earlier that held the 3XL undershirts that would easily cover her.

Dressed in the oversized shirt, Celina climbed up into the bed and tunneled beneath the covers to make a little nest for herself. They had piled several blankets on top of the bed earlier, and though they weighed a ton on top of her, she was grateful for the added layer of protection from the cold night air.

The trials of the day slowly played through her head as she relaxed enough to eventually fall asleep. For once, she didn't dream.

Chapter Five

Early the next morning, Celina woke, trying to remember where she was to be so warm and comfortable. She turned to look for her husband only to remember that he was gone and would never be there to hold and comfort her again. Tears burned her eyes, but she refused to start the day crying. It would drive the direction of her day from there on out.

The need to pee hit her like a bus. She braved the frigid air and climbed out of bed to slip to the floor and race to the bathroom. Thank God she'd slept in her socks. Her feet would have frozen to the floor if she hadn't.

After taking care of her needs and brushing her teeth, she dressed in the only other set of clothes she now owned and carried the lamp downstairs to be ready when she needed it again that night. She noticed that the fire had already been tended to that morning. More than likely both men were already up and about. She had slept better than she had in a long time.

She listened but didn't hear any noises from the kitchen. When she walked through the door, it was to find the room empty, but a pot warming on the stove. She checked and was relieved to find that it was coffee. Even the little community where she had come from didn't always have coffee since it had to be bartered for from the various settlements or rare supply trucks that came through. Abe lived so deep in the Border Lands that she hadn't expected him to have access to it.

She poured some in a cup and sipped at it as she looked out the window over the sink. The early morning light bathed everything in soft colors that teased one into thinking it was a pretty day outside. All she had to do was press her hand to the glass of the window to disprove that illusion. It was cold enough to snow.

The kitchen door leading outside opened, and Abe walked in with a bucket of fresh milk and a basket with eggs. Steam curled from the bucket, confirming it was fresh from the cow. He looked over at her as he stepped out of his boots.

"Good morning, Abe," she offered when he didn't say anything right away.

"Morning. Give me a few minutes and I'll fix something for you to eat." He walked across the room and set the bucket next to the sink and the eggs on the counter.

"Why don't you go and warm up in front of the fire. I'll cook breakfast this morning." She smiled up at him, willing him to smile back.

"You don't have to cook." He didn't offer a return smile.

"I know. I like to cook, so clear out and let me get to work." She made a shooing gesture with her hands.

To her surprise, he took her at her word and left her in the kitchen alone. She just stood there for a second wondering how that had worked out so well. Then it occurred to her that most men didn't like to cook anyway. He was probably relieved to hand it over to her. More than likely he would take it for granted that she would take over the cooking from him. She shrugged. Considering he was giving her a safe place to live, maybe she would.

Thirty minutes later, she had deer steak, gravy, eggs, and biscuits ready. She poked her head through the door to the living area and announced that breakfast was on the table. It didn't take long for the two men to appear in the kitchen. They took their seats and began filling their plates with food. She couldn't stop the smile their enthusiasm created. When they mumbled their approval around mouthfuls of her cooking, she felt a moment of pride that she could at least help with this.

Halfway through the meal, Abe scowled across the table at her. She arched a brow and stared back at him with a questioning look.

"You're supposed to be eating for two. You aren't eating enough to keep you alive, much less feed a baby."

"I'm full. I can't stuff myself, Abe. I'll end up sick at my stomach."

"Then you need to eat snacks spread out all day long. You're not getting enough with what you just ate. Drink another glass of milk."

Russell smiled as he stared down at his plate as if to stay out of the discussion. She wasn't going to let him though.

"Russell, tell Abe I know my own body and when it needs something to eat," she demanded.

He looked up with wide, panic-filled eyes. "Uh, I'm not in this discussion, Celina."

She glared at him. "Coward. You know I'm right."

Abe had the audacity to crack a smile from under his bushy beard. It even reached his usually empty eyes. That irritated her even more. She gritted her teeth and stood up, planning to take her plate to the sink.

"Where are you going?" Abe asked without looking at her.

"What is this? Twenty questions? I'm putting my plate in the sink."

"You haven't poured another glass of milk to drink yet." He took a bite of eggs and settled his steely gaze on her.

"I don't want any more milk right now. I'll drink more later." She took a step away from the table and Abe stopped her with a hand to her arm.

"Drink the milk, Celina." His dark eyes seemed to sparkle in his face. "Please."

It was the please that got her. She nodded her head, and after placing her plate in the sink, she poured another glass of milk and slowly sipped it. She couldn't believe that she was caving to him like this. If he ever did turn on his charm, she'd be a lost cause.

She heard a snicker and turned to find a smiling Russell studiously looking down at his empty plate. She narrowed her eyes at him and returned to the table with deliberate steps. There was no way she would allow either of them to think they could get the best of her. She sat back down and waited for Russell's curiosity to get the better of him. When it did and he looked up, she leveled him with a droll stare.

"I won't forget that you sided with Abe. When you least expect it, Russell. When you least expect it." She got back up and left the two men in the kitchen to finish her milk while sitting in front of the fire.

She hoped they would take the hint and do the dishes. She'd cleaned up behind herself as she cooked, but there were still some to be washed, including the ones they'd eaten from. It was only fair that if she was going to cook, they should clean up afterwards. With that thought, Celina curled her feet underneath her as she sat down on the couch. The fire was a welcome warmth from the surrounding cooler air. At least while she had been cooking, the stove had kept her warm.

Once she'd finished the milk, Celina set the empty glass on the end table and stared into the fire, wondering what she was going to do when the baby came. How could she possibly manage taking care of a baby by herself? She really didn't think that Abe or Russell, for that matter, really wanted her and a child around. They were obviously still hurting from the loss of their families. It really wasn't fair to them for her to hang around once she was well enough to live on her own. All their talk about it not being safe for her to live on her own didn't hide the fact that they didn't want her either.

"Let's go look for some clothes that might fit you." Abe's deep voice startled her.

"Okay." She stood up and followed him back up the stairs and down the long hall to the last room at the end of the hall.

When he opened the door, it was to find an overly large room with a huge bed in the center. The matching bedroom furniture was in need of a good dusting, but it looked to be expensive and well made. A small sitting area was off to one side with a couch and two chairs.

Abe disappeared through one of the doors on one side of the room. Celina followed him to find herself inside a massive walk-in closet. It was overflowing with clothes. He rummaged through them 'til he found what he was looking for.

"I moved all the clothes I found around the place into this room in case I needed them later." He indicated with his hand a section of the area. "This is where the women's clothes start. You can search through and find whatever will fit you. Then look through the shoes. You need another pair of boots, if there are any that will fit."

She nodded but didn't move. He finally grunted and eased past her. She felt his body brush along her back. A small shudder rumbled down her back. What was it about him that sent her libido into overdrive? He was gruff, rude at times, and obviously didn't like her much. Shaking her head, she walked over to the women's clothes and began going through them to see what would fit.

Thirty minutes later, she emerged from the closet with an arm full of clothes and a pair of boots that fit perfectly. She stopped in her tracks when she saw Abe sitting on one of the chairs waiting for her. He slowly stood up before closing the distance between them with long, sure strides. He relieved her of the lamp first then took the clothes from her arms.

"There are other things in the dresser. Go through the drawers and see what you can find." Setting the lamp on the dresser, he carried the clothes and boots from the room.

Celina assumed he was taking them to her room and began opening drawers to see what she could liberate from the dusty piece of furniture. Much to her delight, she found several warm sets of pajamas as well as panties and bras. She hadn't had a bra that actually fit in weeks. No doubt she would need a larger one by the time the baby came.

After taking what she needed, she gathered it up and headed for the door. She couldn't help but wonder why Abe hadn't taken this room for his own. Maybe it was just too big and reminded him of what he had lost. She could totally understand that reasoning. She missed her husband. They'd had their problems, but she had loved him. All couples went through hard times, and considering the world they had found themselves in, they had managed a relatively happy marriage.

Once inside her bedroom, she dropped her new things on the bed and began refolding them as she tucked them into the dresser along with the overly large T-shirts for sleeping. She noticed that Abe had left the boots in front of the closet door. She hung up the three dresses she'd found in her size along with the pants and jeans then tucked the boots in the closet as well.

"How are you doing?" Russell poked his head through the doorway from the hall.

"Hey. I just finished putting everything away. What are you up to?"

"I was wondering if you want to play a game of checkers. I have the board set up downstairs."

Celina smiled. That sounded like fun to her. She couldn't remember the last time she'd played.

"I'd love to. I'm rusty though. You'll have to be patient." She smiled and let him lead her through the door and down the stairs.

"It's just checkers, not chess. There's no real thinking behind it," he teased.

"There is if you want to win, and I plan on winning." She gave him her haughtiest look.

Russell surprised her by bursting out laughing. He indicated one of the chairs at the small makeshift game table he had set up in front of the fire. The board was already set up for a game. It looked as if she would have the white pieces. She looked around but didn't see Abe anywhere.

"Where is Abe?"

"He went out to check on the animals. Said it's going to snow later tonight." Russell settled into his chair and looked up at her expectantly. "You get to go first."

They had just gotten into their game when the door across the room opened, letting in a rush of cold air. Abe stepped in after stomping off his boots just outside the door. After closing and bolting the door, he shrugged out of his outerwear and hung it up. He walked toward them and stepped in front of the fireplace, holding his hands out to the flickering flames.

"Everything okay out there?" Russell asked as he studied the board.

"Fine."

Celina almost sighed out loud at the clipped answer. He didn't seem to want to interact with them most of the time. She was surprised that he had even come back inside so soon. If the weather hadn't been so cold, she doubted he would have. As much as that bothered her, what bothered her even more was that he seemed so lost and empty sometimes. It was almost as if he didn't know how to communicate anymore. She struggled to think of something to say to him, but nothing came to mind.

"Your move." Russell drew her attention back to the game.

"Who's winning?" Abe's deep voice sounded almost hoarse from disuse.

"I am, of course," she said with a laugh.

"I'm just letting her win so she'll make lunch." Russell grinned at her.

"She doesn't have to cook if she doesn't want to." Abe scowled at the other man.

"Don't worry, Abe. I like to cook, and he's losing because I'm just better than him."

Russell gave her a mock scowl that had her almost giggling. When she looked up, the expression on Abe's face almost broke her heart. Then it was gone and she could almost believe she had imagined it. For a few seconds, he'd looked at them as if he wanted to be included in their teasing. His eyes held a longing so deep it should have taken him to his knees, but then it was gone and the gruff stranger was back with his almost empty stare. It made her shiver to see such a difference in an instant.

Abe turned and walked out of the room. It took all of her strength to keep from getting up and following him. The need that had been in his eyes had nearly broken her heart. She looked over at Russell and realized he was watching her with a curious expression on his face.

"Okay, Russell. Prepare to lose." Celina refocused on the game.

Fifteen minutes later, she took the winning piece from him and laughed when he pouted.

"I better get started on lunch. Do you have any preferences for dinner tonight?" she asked him.

"Naw. Anything you cook will be good. I'll clean up this. I expect a rematch tomorrow."

She chuckled and agreed before walking into the kitchen. It didn't take her long to throw together a quick meal. Then she started the prep for soup for dinner. She had just browned the meat and set it aside when Abe walked into the room. She continued what she was doing as he sat down at the table.

"Is Russell on his way or should I call him?"

"He's on his way. He went to wash up."

She glanced over her shoulder at him before washing her hands at the sink and joining him at the table. He passed the plate of sandwiches to her before dipping into the jar of pickles.

"I can't believe you started without me." Russell's huffed out breath drew a smile to her face.

"Should have gotten here on time. Better hope we left enough for you." Celina bit her lip to keep from laughing.

They quickly ate, leaving nothing but a half-empty jar of pickles behind. Russell volunteered to wash the dishes while she continued working on dinner. By the time she had the soup simmering on the stove and the biscuit dough ready to cut, she was alone in the kitchen. She wondered over to the window and stared sightlessly through it as she thought about Abe and how much he seemed to want more than what he had.

Celina gave a half laugh at that thought. They all wanted more than what they had. Each of them had lost their other half and had to cope without them. It wasn't lost on her that both men probably deep down resented her a little bit because she was alive and their wives and families weren't. She could just about say the same thing about them, except that they had saved her and given her baby a chance at life.

She ran her hand over her slightly rounded abdomen. She figured her child would be born sometime around the end of February or the beginning of March. Of course with everything that had happened in the last few weeks, she wasn't real sure what month it was now. If she gave birth toward the end of winter, then by the end of spring, she could possibly talk them into letting her live in one of the cabins. She grinned sadly. A few months of living with a screaming baby would surely give her the edge she would need to get them to agree.

Coming back to the present, she noticed how dark it was getting outside. Heavy clouds were building up, supporting Abe's claim there would be snow soon. She turned back to the stove and checked the soup before rubbing her hands up and down her arms and returning to the great room where the fire was. Both men sat in chairs on either side of the couch.

"You were right, Abe. It looks like snow out there." She settled herself on the couch.

"It's going to be a bad one." Abe stretched in the chair but didn't get up.

"Do you want help with the cows after dinner?" Russell asked.

"Wouldn't turn it down. It will go faster with two of us."

"Is there anything I can do?" she asked.

"Stay inside. Don't need you catching cold out there." Abe didn't look in her direction. "How long until dinner's ready?"

"It should be ready in another hour if you want to eat soon. I imagine it will be dark outside anyway. Why don't you see to the animals first while there's still some light?"

"She's got a point, Abe. It will be easier if we go ahead before it gets completely dark." Russell leaned forward in his chair.

Abe sighed and stood up. "Let's go. We need to bring some wood in on the way back. I'm not sure how cold it will actually get, but we're in for a good amount of snow."

As they bundled up to go outside, Celina wondered what was going on inside of Abe's head. He'd looked reluctant to move and yet he'd been the one to want to take care of the animals as early in the day as possible. She didn't know enough about either man to try to understand them, but she wanted to. They were going to be living with each other for the next few months, so knowing more about them would make things a lot easier in the long run. One thing marriage to her husband had taught her was to learn everything she could about another person in order to avoid their triggers.

Triggers had a habit of blowing up on you if you weren't careful. Celina had every intention of being careful.

Chapter Six

Abe smothered a curse as he banged his hand against the gate, trying to get the fucking latch back on it. He was glad Russell had pushed to go ahead and take care of the animals early. Normally he would have been out there right after lunch anyway, but the last twenty-four hours had taken a toll on him. For nearly eight years he'd been alone, and after the first year, had managed to close his memories off for the most part. All it had taken was one day for Celina to open the Pandora's box of his past to wreak havoc in his world.

Her smiles ate at the chains he'd placed around his heart as her beauty awakened another part of him he hadn't really paid much attention to in years. It disgusted him that he would even think about her in that way when she was a new widow and expecting another man's child. What did that make him?

"Got the horses taken care of. Need help out here?" Russell was shouting over the wind that had begun to pick up.

"Cows are fine for the night. We'll need to see about them in the morning if it snows much by then." He looked up at the heavy clouds that almost seemed to undulate as he watched. "Let's carry a few logs up to the porch before we go back inside."

Russell followed him out to where he chopped wood all during the summer in preparation for winter. They made several trips each before calling it a night and heading inside. As soon as he had hung up his coat and hat, Abe walked over to the hearth and shared the warmth with the other man. They didn't say anything, just stood there letting the fire warm their frozen bodies. He could hear noises coming from the kitchen that told him Celina was in there finishing up dinner. That knowledge seemed to settle him some, deep inside.

"How far are we from a town or city that might still have some things in their stores?" Russell asked out of the blue.

"Huh?" He looked over at the other man. "Why?"

"I think that if we get a clear day, one of us needs to go and see if we can find any baby things we might need before we can't go anywhere."

"Fuck." He didn't want to think about that.

Thinking about her bearing a child sent chills down his spine. He didn't know a damn thing about birthing a baby, and he didn't want to picture her with one.

"There's a small town about two-hour's drive from here." He sighed and shook his head. "I'm going to go wash up before dinner."

With that, he walked off, leaving Russell in front of the fireplace. He was sure the other man thought him to be heartless where the woman was concerned, but he didn't want to think about her that way right now. He was still trying to adjust to her even being there. Hell, he wasn't quite resigned to Russell living there yet.

Abe liked Russell. He'd worked to pull his weight even before he should have been up and about. He wasn't a lazy man by any means. His one fault, as far as Abe was concerned, was that he allowed himself to feel too much.

With a snort, he stripped down to bare skin in the chilly bedroom and strode into the bathroom to shower off. He glanced over at the other sink where Celina had left her female things, a brush, her toothbrush, and a hair clasp. Seeing them lying there jerked at something deep inside of him. He turned away and adjusted the shower as he stepped inside. Thoughts of her played across his mind's eye like a trailer for a movie years ago. He couldn't stop them, and soon he was imagining her without her clothes.

"Hell." He quickly ducked his head under the stream of water and washed his face.

Thinking like that about her was a sure way to damnation. She wasn't available to him like that. Not just because she was pregnant, but because she had only recently lost her husband. Besides, she was a good woman. She didn't deserve to be treated like an easy lay. Sex was all he could offer. There wasn't anything human or normal left inside of him to offer her even if she was open to more.

"Russell will be a good man for her once she's had time to grieve."

He quickly finished his shower and turned off the water. He needed to dry off and dress before one of them called up that dinner was ready. He glanced at his semierect cock and winced at the thought of stuffing it into a pair of jeans. The chill of the air outside of the shower had helped calm him down some, but it hadn't fully taken care of the issue. He should have jacked off in the shower instead of fighting it.

Just as he walked out of his bedroom, Celina entered the hallway. His dick stiffened, and he was thankful he'd decided on warm ups until he realized his arousal would be noticeable. Gritting his teeth, Abe stepped to the middle of the hall.

"I'm on my way down."

"Good. I was just coming to tell you that dinner is ready." She smiled at him as she drew closer to him.

Abe wanted to tell her to stop before the light from her lantern revealed his problem. Instead, he stood his ground and waited for her to draw closer.

"I'm on my way down."

She smiled and had just started to turn back around to leave when her eyes snagged on the front of his jogging pants. She froze. Her eyes widened then drifted almost shut as she licked her lips. Just as suddenly her eyes shot back to his with some expression he couldn't read. Then she turned and hurried back toward the stairs.

"Slow down, Celina, so you don't fall. I'll be down in a minute." He wanted to give them both a few minutes to settle down before he joined them in the kitchen.

She didn't say anything, but she did slow her gait as she descended the stairs. It took him a good three minutes to rein in his desire and bury it under a will of iron. At least he hoped it was still made of iron. God knew he needed it. Having her wary around him wasn't a bad thing, but it ate at him. If he were honest with himself, deep down, Abe didn't want her to fear him. An ache bloomed that he had no doubt would soon grow into something much worse before spring. How he was going to endure it, he didn't know.

He tended to the fire in the great room before he finally made himself walk into the kitchen. Russell and Celina were already at the table, ladling soup into their bowls. There was also a plate of fluffy biscuits and various jellies to choose from, as well. Seeing the two of them sitting together so easily burned in his gut. He quickly beat down the resentment and reminded himself that he wasn't interested. She was too young for both of them, but Russell seemed to be in better emotional shape than he was.

"This is good, Celina. You're a great cook." Russell's praise seemed to bring a shine to her face.

Abe agreed with Russell and managed to say as much without growling. It was a miracle that he was able to force out a single word with the tightness in his throat.

"Do you want some more, Abe?" Celina stood up and started around the table with the pot of soup.

"I'll get it." He quickly stood up and took the pot from her. "It's too heavy for you to be carrying around like that."

She let him take the pot but then picked up the biscuits and set them down near him before carrying her empty bowl and plate to the sink. He couldn't stop his eyes from following her every move. When he started to look back at his plate, his gaze caught Russell watching him with a thoughtful expression on his face.

"What?" he demanded in a gruff voice.

"Nothing. I'm going to take my shower now. Mind helping her with the dishes tonight?"

Before Abe could make an excuse, Russell was standing up and carrying his plate to the sink. He heard the other man tell Celina how good it was and that he was going to shower. Then he walked out of the room with a smile on his face. No doubt the quick peck on her cheek had something to do with that.

As soon as he finished, Abe jumped up and added his dishes to the sink. Celina had been busily putting away the leftover soup for the next day. It would be safe enough as cold as it got in the pantry at night.

"I'll wash and you can dry now that you know where things go." Abe filled the sink with water.

As they worked together in silence, he couldn't help wishing that life was different. This quiet time was probably the closest he'd been to contentment that in a long time. The fact that it was largely due to the fact that there was a female at his side wasn't lost on him. Yes, having Russell around to help with the chores was an added bonus as well, but there was something about Celina and her easy spirit that settled something inside of him. It should worry him, but at the moment, it didn't. He would allow worry to come later when he was alone in his bed.

"Thank you for helping with the dishes, Abe. Made it go much faster." She smiled up at him while she dried the last glass.

Abe took it from her and set it on the shelf in the cabinet over her head. He had to bite back the hiss of awareness that shocked him anytime their skin touched.

"No need for you to be on your feet any longer than you have to be. You cooked for us."

"I told you that I don't mind. I really like to cook, and you two eat enough to make it worth it." She smiled again, but this time it was in amusement.

"Are you saying we eat too much?"

"Not at all. Just that you seem to enjoy what you eat, and that makes it fun to cook."

Abe realized he was flirting with her and scowled before turning away. "I'm going to bring in more wood so it won't be wet in the morning when we need it."

He could feel her eyes on him as he stomped out of the room. No doubt he'd hurt her feelings. The sooner she realized he wasn't someone to try to be friends with, the better. Nothing would ever become of it. He'd make sure she was safe, but anything more than that would only be asking for trouble and heartache. He'd had enough of that to last him a lifetime.

* * * *

Celina watched Abe walk away. What had happened? One minute they had been talking like friends, and the next he was growling and seemed almost angry. What had she said wrong? No matter how many times she went over their brief conversation, she couldn't figure it out. Resigned to never knowing what had triggered his sudden about-face, she wiped down the counters and table before walking into the other room.

Russell sat in one of the lounge chairs while Abe was fiddling with the fire. There was a mountain of logs piled on a tarp next to the hearth now. Abe obviously felt that they were in for a major storm by the looks of it. She ventured over to the window that looked out into the back of the lodge. When she peered through the heavy drapes that helped to insulate the windows, it took a few seconds for her eyes to adjust to the deep darkness outside the firelit room.

A thin covering of snow covered the ground outside, and as she watched, more floated down to add to it. It wasn't a blizzard by any means, but it was definitely coming down. She thought it beautiful for a little while before the reality of what it meant returned to taunt her.

It made feeding the animals and caring for them much more difficult. It brought colder air that would make it more difficult to heat the lodge.

She turned away from the deceptive beauty and hurried over to the couch where she could warm up near the fire. Suddenly she was much more aware of how cold she'd gotten standing there.

"Still coming down out there?" Russell asked.

"Yeah. Not really hard, but steady."

"That will change. We're in for a hard one. I just hope the temperatures stay in the twenties and don't dip much lower." Abe had abandoned the fireplace and was sitting in his chair now.

"How much snow do you think we'll get?" She hoped it wouldn't be too deep. The men had to be able to get back and forth to the barn and pasture.

"I'm hoping not much more than three feet," Abe said.

She hissed out a breath. That was deeper than what she was used to. How could they possibly handle working in that? She would need to keep warm food ready for them. They would need hearty meals to keep up their strength and stay warm.

"Were you warm enough sleeping last night, Celina?" Russell asked with a worried frown.

"Yes. I was fine. Didn't want to venture out from my warm nest this morning. I expect it will be even harder to make myself get up in the morning."

"If you need more covers, there are plenty more piled on the bed in one of the other rooms." Abe's brows furrowed as if he hadn't thought about it before.

"No, thanks, I'm fine right now. I guess if it gets much colder, I'll need them, but I'm fine for now."

"I'm heading up to bed." Abe stood up and strode from the room.

She didn't turn to watch him climb the stairs. Instead, she stared into the dancing flames of the fire and wondered what it would take to get him to relax more around them. He seemed so lonely inside, and yet he worked at keeping them at arm's length.

"How are you holding up?" Russell's calm words made her smile.

"I'm doing fine, Russell. What about you? How's your back and shoulders?"

"They're pretty much healed up. Shoulder is a little stiff when I first get up in the morning, but it loosens up quickly enough."

"Abe is so distant, almost withdrawn. I hate seeing him like that."

"He's much more open than when I first woke up here. There were days when he didn't so much as grunt around me. Give him time to get used to having you around. He's basically been alone out here for eight years. I'm sure being around people again takes some getting used to."

Celina nodded. Russell was right. It had only been a few days. Besides being another human being encroaching on his sanctuary, she was a woman as well. Then she placed her hand on her belly and smiled. A pregnant woman. It would be a lot for someone like him to deal with.

She frowned as another thought entered her mind. What if her presence there would only remind him of what he'd lost and be a constant source of pain to him? How could she stand that? She looked over at Russell. He'd lost his family as well. How did he feel about her being there? It was a lot to think about. She stood up to head to bed as well. She didn't think she wanted to think about something like that around Russell.

"I'm glad you're here, Celina. Don't worry so much about us. We'll be fine. You have more to think about than to waste time worrying about us. Get some rest, sweetie."

She managed a nervous smile before she hurried to her room. She bundled into the pajamas and snuggled under the covers, shivering until her little nest warmed with her body heat. Russell was right. She shouldn't let their emotions play on hers so much. She needed to remain as calm as possible for her baby. She had a lot ahead of her with winter settling in and a future to plan. Whether or not Abe and Russell would be in it or not was yet to be revealed. She liked the two men, and they had been so good to her that she hoped they would always be around as friends.

Friends and maybe more?

She shivered at that thought. Where had it come from? She squelched it and settled down to sleep.

Chapter Seven

"Durn!" Celina scowled at the counter where she'd hit her head when she'd bent over to retrieve her brush.

The opposite door to the bathroom swung open with a thump against the wall. Abe stood there with worried expression on his face. She stood there in just her pajamas, shivering as she held her hand over her head were she'd hit it. Their eyes met in the mirror.

"Are you okay? What did you do?" He stepped into the small room and grabbed her wrist in his big hand. "Let me see."

"It's nothing. I just hit my head on the counter when I dropped my brush."

He moved her hand away from her forehead and frowned. "You've got a red spot, but it's not bleeding."

She tried to step back, but stumbled. Abe grabbed her around her waist and jerked her toward him. Their bodies collided, and it took all of her concentration not to gasp and jerk free. He felt so warm next to her. He wore thermal underwear and nothing else. She was well aware of his arousal pressed against lower belly. The clingy material had left nothing to the imagination as she'd noticed before he'd pulled her into his arms.

As if realizing what he'd revealed to her, Abe quickly stepped back, leaving a hand on her waist until he was sure she was able to stand without help. Then he backed farther away and stood in the doorway to his room once again.

"Be more careful. Get dressed before you catch cold." He turned and closed the door behind him.

Celina realized she'd been holding her breath when a wave of dizziness washed over her. She let out the breath and took several deep ones to regain her sanity. What had just happened? Despite the frigid air around her, her face was on fire as was the rest of her body. She quickly finished in the bathroom and dressed in the bedroom before heading for the kitchen.

She set the lantern on the counter and quickly set up the pot for coffee before looking out the window to a sight that brought both wonder and fear. There was at least three feet of snow if not more, and it was still coming down hard. Not only that, but the wind made it almost horizontal in its descent. With the cloud cover, dawn wouldn't give much light for the men to work by.

Turning away, she quickly started breakfast while her mind tortured her with thoughts of Abe in those thermals, holding her tightly against his very aroused body. Why did that make her feel so hot and uncomfortable? It wasn't right for her to feel this way while she was carrying Roger's baby.

A noise from the great room pulled her back from her naughty thoughts. She pulled a mug down from the cabinet and filled it with coffee before going into the other room. Abe stood in front of the fire, using a poker to maneuver a log where he wanted it in the building fire. She couldn't help but admire how the muscles of his back and shoulders bunched and rippled as he manhandled the stubborn piece of wood. Her pussy grew moist, and that quickly snapped her thoughts back to the present.

"Here's some coffee, Abe." She stepped closer and held the cup out to him.

He turned and accepted it, watching her closely as if waiting for her to say or do something that would piss him off. No doubt he expected her to either berate him for what had happened earlier or try to elicit another situation like it. She swallowed at that thought and took a step back. He didn't follow her with his body, but his eyes didn't release hers.

"Thanks. Looks like there are going to be another couple of feet before this blows over." He watched her eyes widen before she could stop her mind from taking his words the wrong way.

"The snow. It's coming down hard out there."

Celina almost groaned at the images that one word elicited. She regained control of herself once again and took another step back.

"Breakfast will be ready in a few more minutes. Is Russell up yet?"

"He was in the shower when I came down. We'll be in to eat in a few minutes." He had turned back to the fire so that she couldn't see his face.

Celina hurried back to the safety of the kitchen to finish the meal. When the kitchen door opened ten minutes later, she didn't turn around to see if both men had arrived. Instead she dished up the food and steeled herself to remain calm as she faced the table and the two men sitting there waiting on her. She quickly added the dishes to the table and joined them.

Since it was so early and no one had been out to collect eggs or milk the cow yet, they were eating lunch foods instead of breakfast ones. She would cook breakfast for lunch instead.

Nothing was said all during the meal. Their silence made her nervous. She wasn't used to so much quiet. It had never been quiet around her homes. Even during the last few years, she and her husband had talked about everything. This new life would take some getting used to. She didn't mind it so much, except that she felt like it wasn't an easy silence. It felt rife with tension and worry. Whether that was due to the snow or her presence, she didn't know.

Russell and Abe finished eating and stood up. They carried their plates to the sink and poured another cup of coffee. Celina was still eating when they finished it and headed for the other room.

"I'll bring the eggs and milk in as soon as I can. We're going to work on the herd first, though." Abe's voice as he walked through the door did little to reassure her.

Before she could answer, the door swung shut behind them. She sighed and quickly cleaned up the kitchen, washing the dishes as fast as she could so she could return to the great room and the warm fire. Before she did, though, she located the insulated thermos and travel mugs she'd found and washed the day before. When Abe returned, she would send him back out with a thermos of coffee and filled cups.

The fire slowly warmed her chilled body and she settled onto the couch to plan the day. When Abe opened the door almost an hour later, she nearly yelped in surprise. She followed him to the kitchen and started pouring up the coffee.

"We'll be another hour or so outside." He turned to go, but she stopped him.

"Wait. Take this with you." She thrust the thermos and two insulated cups toward him. "It will help keep you warm while you're out there. I'll make more coffee in an hour for when you return. Be careful."

Abe's eyes widened for an instant. Then he nodded and gave her a gruff *thank you* before turning away to shoulder through the kitchen door. Celina followed him and helped open the outside door for him. Once it was once again closed, she looked at the melted snow trail from the door to the kitchen and went in search of the mop to clean up the mess.

Once that was done, she tended to the milk and eggs. By the time she had everything taken care of in the kitchen, she had to add a log to the fire before it went out. She tried to keep busy to keep her mind off of thinking about the men out in the bitter cold in three feet of snow. Or was it four feet now? She had noticed when Abe had gone out earlier that it was piled up on either side of the door where they'd obviously shoveled a path to the outbuildings.

By the time they returned, she was back in the kitchen, brewing coffee for them. She heard them when they stomped off their boots outside the door before closing the door behind them. She could imagine them removing their gloves, scarves, coats, and hats before hurrying over to stand in front of the fire to get warm. She quickly poured up the coffee and carried it into the other room.

They both looked up when she walked into the room. The heat in their gazes sent her hormones into a gallop. Her pussy grew wet as her nipples peaked beneath the layers of clothes she was wearing. Before she had made it to where they were standing, they'd regained control once more. They accepted the cups without speaking and avoided looking her in the eyes. Celina grabbed the now-empty thermos and cups off of the end table and carried them back to the kitchen with her.

She realized in that moment that regardless of their pasts, despite their resolve, and no matter how honorable they were, none of them would be able to escape the heat building between them. Eventually they would act on it. All that remained uncertain was how they would react to it. Celina closed her eyes as she leaned against the counter with her back to the door. Did she want this—them? She honestly didn't know. All she knew was that she had loved Roger, but he was gone and she was left with a baby on the way to care for and raise.

Deep down she knew that they wouldn't force her, but they would probably seduce her. She held no illusions that they couldn't, based on her reactions to them already. She could either accept it for what it was and be thankful they were willing to let her stay with them, or she could fight it and make them all uncomfortable.

She still held some reservations about what she would do once winter was over with and her baby a month or so old. Unless Abe relaxed more around her during the coming months, Celina didn't think she could live with them on a permanent basis. The stress would be too hard to deal with, and she didn't want her child to be subject to it.

Closing her eyes, she prayed that she would make the right decision when the time came for one of the two she knew was ahead of her. She didn't expect there to be love or anything more than a mutual respect between them since they'd all had families once. Still, the woman in her wanted more than it to be just sex. Emotions were a major part of the female makeup. She could see Russell caring about her, and that would be enough, but Abe? She just didn't know if there was anything still alive inside of him capable of feeling something other than emptiness.

Celina hoped there was. No one should have to exist without some form of passion inside of them. Even though a piece of her died with Roger, there was still enough of her left to care about these two men who had taken her in. Only time would tell if it was enough to form a bond or not. Until then, she planned to make sure they always felt cared for regardless of their feelings toward her.

* * * *

Russell stretched as he stood up from the chair. Immediately, cold air snaked around his warm back end, seeping beneath his clothes to bite at his skin. It had obviously grown colder since they'd finished dinner earlier. He knew it had felt colder that afternoon when they had returned outside to shovel the snow before it grew too deep to walk in. If he could feel this cold sitting in front of the fire, it was going to be bitter cold upstairs to try to sleep.

"Abe, it feels a lot colder than a few hours ago." He eased closer to the fire.

"I was afraid it would get colder once the clouds were gone." He bit off a curse as he glanced toward Celina.

Russell noticed she had fallen asleep curled up on the couch with a thick blanket covering her up to her neck. He looked back at Abe. The other man stood up and walked over to the window to look out around the foam-backed curtain. The man placed the back of his hand against the glass pane. He quickly removed it and returned to stand in front of the fire with him.

"It's cold enough that sleeping alone upstairs isn't going to work. We need to drag one of the mattresses down here in front of the fire. We'll have to sleep together to share body heat."

Russell could tell that the other man didn't like the idea one bit. He wondered why it was so repugnant to him. Granted that he would rather not have to share a bed with them either, but it wasn't a fate worse than death, and Abe seemed to be taking it that way. He nodded and followed the other man upstairs where they chose a room with a king-size mattress and helped him drag it, complete with bed sheets and covers, down the stairs to the great room.

"We'll need to move the couch back and put the mattress in the middle close to the fire."

Russell followed Abe's lead as they gently moved the couch back so they could fit the massive mattress between the two recliners. They made sure to leave plenty of room between the bed and the fireplace so that they could tend to the fire during the night without falling over the mattress.

"What's going on?" Celina's sleepy voice stopped them as they straightened the bedclothes and added another blanket to the two already on it.

"The temperature has dropped enough that sleeping upstairs is out of the question now." Abe didn't look in her direction as he answered her question.

"Oh." She didn't expand on that.

Russell finished his side of the makeshift bed and collapsed on the couch next to her. The covers had slipped from her neck to pool in her lap. Despite the fact that she had on a couple of layers of clothes, there was no disguising her pebbled nipples. He found his eyes drawn to them despite his resolve to stop.

As if oblivious to the fact both he and Abe were staring at her breasts, Celina stood up and dropped the blankets back on the couch.

"I'm going to put on my pajamas. I'll be back down in a few minutes."

Russell watched her go, his need to follow her almost overwhelming him. Instead he pulled the blankets she'd abandoned toward him. Her scent teased him as he wrapped them around his body. She smelled of vanilla and cinnamon. Nothing she had fixed for lunch or dinner had boasted either one of those flavors that he was aware of. The scent had to be unique to her.

"This is going to be hell."

He heard the words despite the fact Abe had pretty much whispered them. No doubt he hadn't meant to say them out loud.

"Maybe, but she would end up sick if we don't do this."

Abe's head jerked up to stare at him. No, the big man hadn't meant to say them out loud. His eyes narrowed before he closed his eyes and drew in a deep breath.

"I moved out here where there wasn't anyone for a reason," he said with a growl.

"I did the same thing. Looks like neither one of us got what we wanted, but maybe we got what we needed anyway."

"The hell, you say. She isn't looking for anyone for anything more than keeping her alive."

"Are you saying you want more from her?" Russell knew he was pulling the tiger's tail, but Abe needed to face the fact that he wasn't alone anymore and like it or not, Celina was a woman.

Russell knew she had just lost her husband, but she was pregnant and he remembered how emotional his wife had been when she had been carrying their children. Everything would affect her stronger than usual, and Abe needed to tone down his standoffish behavior. Since he thought the other man was hiding his attraction to the woman behind it, that meant getting him to face some things.

"I–I didn't say that," he snapped back.

"You didn't have to. It's written all over you when you look at her. Hell, you've had a hard-on almost since she arrived."

"Doesn't mean anything." Abe turned away to face the fire.

"Right." Russell shook his head. The man was nothing if not stubborn.

The sound of shoes coming down the stairs stopped him from saying more. Instead, Russell waited for her to join them. When she did, he had to swallow and will his cock to be still. She had let her hair down from the ponytail she'd worn it in all day. The golden tresses glowed in the firelight. She had on a pair of soft-looking pajamas with kittens chasing after balls of yarn and a pair of socks. She'd wrapped a blanket around her shoulders to keep her warm on the walk back to the great room.

"Ready for bed?" Russell stood up and took the lantern from her.

"Yeah. I'm really tired. I woke up too early this morning, I think."

Russell lifted one side of the covers so she could climb on the mattress. She smiled her thanks and dropped her blanket to crawl across the mattress.

"Stick to the middle, Celina. We'll sleep on either side of you." Abe finally spoke up from the other side of the bed.

She stopped and moved around until she seemed comfortable. He caught a fleeting expression slide across her face before it disappeared and was replaced with a serene smile. For an instant, uncertainty filled her eyes. He hoped she would be able to fall asleep fairly quickly. Otherwise, they would all feed off of each other's nervousness and none of them would get any rest.

Abe peeled off his jeans and shirt until he stood in a pair of thermals. He too left his socks on. Russell began removing his jeans as the other man climbed under the covers, turning his back to them. Once Russell was down to thermals, he slipped in, turning his back to them as well. He doubted any of them touched at all. Hopefully the body heat would still combine to keep them all warm.

As he lay trying not to think about Celina just a few inches behind him, Russell allowed his thoughts to drift in hopes he'd fall asleep soon. They had a long, hard day ahead of them the next day, since the frigid cold would turn the snow to ice, making it much harder to walk in and shovel. Even as that thought kicked in, his skin began to warm to a more reasonable temperature. Together with an uncensored image of Celina lying nude beneath him, his cock grew hard and he drifted off into sleep to dream about the woman and different ways to keep her warm.

Chapter Eight

Celina opened her eyes, filled with the need to get up and start breakfast. Immediately she remembered that they were all sleeping downstairs in front of the fire. She became aware that she wasn't on a soft mattress anymore, though. A muscular shoulder pillowed her head and her body was wrapped around Abe's body. She knew it was Abe because of the sheer size of the chest she was hugging.

Dear, God. One leg was thrown over his and she had her knee close to his groin while she seemed to be pressed tightly against his leg with her crotch. To say that her underwear was soaked was an understatement. What in the world had she been dreaming about?

When she started to move away from Abe, she realized that Russell was right behind her with a hand over her waist and his leg lying across hers. She wasn't going anywhere until one of them woke up. The idea of them waking up to find them fitted together like a puzzle had heat burning her cheeks.

She closed her eyes and relaxed once again. She would enjoy the closeness and feeling of belonging while she had it. In reality it meant nothing to anyone, but she would take advantage of the illusion that everything was fine for now.

"Uh, Celina?" Russell's voice whispered in her ear. "Are you awake?"

Her eyes popped open. "Yes, but I'm scared to move."

She felt him slowly extract himself from around her before he scooted over in the bed. She sighed and started to move away from Abe, but his arm around her upper back and the one holding her hip tightened.

"Where are you going?" Abe's voice sounded husky.

"Abe, it's Celina." She figured he was thinking about his wife and not her.

"I know. Where are you going?" he asked again.

"I was going to start coffee and something to eat."

"Too early. We can't go outside yet anyway. Rest a little longer." He tightened his hold on her.

Mortified by the fact that her wet crotch lay against his thermal-covered leg, she almost insisted he let her go. Before she could open her mouth to tell him she needed to get up anyway, Russell returned to his position at her back. She was trapped between them now. Somehow it didn't make her nervous as much as uncomfortable. Their positions were much too suggestive for her peace of mind.

"Sleep, Celina." Abe nuzzled her hair before dropping a kiss on her forehead.

She lay there wondering what to make of everything. Why was he okay with their close proximity now when before he'd done everything he could to avoid her? Even the way he spoke had acted like a buffer between them. Confusion swirled in her head and heart. She was old enough to know that her obvious arousal didn't mean she was being disloyal to her husband's memory. She had loved Roger. What worried her about it was that Abe didn't really want her.

The big man had made it obvious that he barely tolerated her presence there in his home. Why would he want to hold her and be near her now? A sickening thought filled her mind. He might be pretending to himself that she was his dead wife. She immediately chastised herself. So what if he was. Hadn't she been taking advantage of it just a few seconds ago? Who was she to begrudge him comfort if that was what it was to him?

Yet for some reason, it hurt just a little bit. She wanted him to like her and relax some around her. She didn't like feeling like an imposition or a burden that he had to bear. She was afraid that no matter how much she might help around the house and later, in the garden, he would still see her as an added responsibility that he hadn't asked for. What could she do to alter his perception of her presence there?

Several minutes later, Abe sighed and released his hold on her. It was obvious that he wasn't happy—as usual.

"Might as well get up. You're thinking so hard over there I can hear the wheels turn." He moved as soon as she moved off of him.

When she started to scoot across the mattress to stand up, he stopped her.

"Stay there until I get the fire built back up. It's too cold for you to be out from under the covers right now."

She didn't argue since he was right. It was colder than anything she'd ever felt before out from under the covers. She pulled them back up to her neck and waited for the room around her to warm some.

"I'll get the coffee started," Russell said.

She watched him pull his jeans on over the thermals before buttoning up a long-sleeve shirt. He winked at her then walked toward the kitchen. She turned to watch as Abe added logs to the fire. Once he had it like he wanted, he turned back to look down at her.

"Stay there for another fifteen or twenty minutes. The room should warm up enough for you to be able to stand it. I'm going to go find some jeans and a shirt for you. You should bring your clothes down here to dress in the mornings."

"Thanks. I didn't think about that."

"Guess you wouldn't have if you haven't lived in this climate before." He walked off before she said anything else.

She heard his heavy tread on the stairs as he climbed to the second floor. A few minutes later, she heard him return down the stairs. She looked up when he stepped into view. He didn't say anything, just dropped some clothes on the couch and headed toward the kitchen. She hoped he'd gotten something that would be warm enough and look decent together. Even if they were the only ones who would see her, she liked to at least not clash if she could help it.

Everything was different now, not only was the world she had grown up in gone, but so was everyone she had ever loved. She had found herself among strangers who had taken her in and offered her safety and even friendship. All she had to offer was her ability to cook. Looking decent seemed trivial when all was said and done, but it gave her some sense of control over her life when she felt as if she had none. It reminded her that she was a woman and not just a burden.

After a while, she decided it had been long enough. There was no way to tell time without a working watch. Self-winding watches were hard to come by, and those that required batteries were a waste, since she couldn't get a replacement battery.

Celina took the chance that the men wouldn't venture back into the great room and quickly stripped and dressed once again. Her outfit that Abe had picked out was indeed warm and looked fairly good together. She straightened the bed and hurried into the kitchen to start breakfast. Abe was still inside when she walked through the door. He nodded as he drank his coffee, looking out the window.

When she pulled down a cup to pour her own coffee, Abe stopped her with a hand on her arm.

"Best not to be drinking coffee. The caffeine isn't good for the baby. Should have said something before now, but I didn't think about it."

She scowled at the big man. Deep down she knew he was right, but she really could use the coffee to help stay warm. She sighed and put the cup back before diving into preparing breakfast.

"I'm heading out now. One of us will be back in with the milk and eggs as soon as we can. It's going to take some work to get the doors open with the snow frozen now."

"I think that while it's so cold and hard to get to the milk and eggs, I'm going to keep moving breakfast foods to lunch time and make soup and sandwiches for breakfast."

Abe nodded without saying anything more. He strode through the door into the great room to dress to go out in the frigid cold. Celina worried about them out there so much, but there were no other options. The work had to be done or they would starve. She was thankful that she had a warm place and a roof over her head. She owed Abe a lot and needed to constantly remind herself of that. There were few men out there now who wouldn't have taken advantage of her situation. With one more glance at the coffee, she gritted her teeth and got to work on the meal. They would need a hot one when they returned.

* * * *

Abe stretched out in the recliner in front of the fire, relieved that they hadn't lost any of the cows to the bitter cold so far. He and Russell had worked hard all day making sure the herd had plenty to eat and were staying close together so their body heat would help keep each other warm. The deadly cold had been hell to work in, but thanks to Celina, they had a constant supply of hot coffee and hearty meals. He had to admit that finding the thermos and those travel mugs had been a godsend. Knowing that she worried about them and had tried to find a way to make them more comfortable said a lot about her personality and innate compassion and thoughtfulness.

He opened his eyes to look at her as she sat bundled up on the couch. She hadn't complained about being cold even though he knew that despite the warmth from the stove, the kitchen wasn't as warm as the great room was in front of the fire. He needed to double-check the bedrooms for thermals that would fit her. She could use them under her clothes. Of course, as she grew, they wouldn't fit anymore. He frowned. He didn't like thinking about her being pregnant. It reminded him of what he'd lost.

Let it go, Abe. It's been over eight years. Time to move on.

Still, a part of him didn't want to forget his family. They deserved to be remembered. They'd loved him as much as he had loved them. He wiped a hand over his face. Dwelling on it wasn't healthy, though. It occurred to him that maybe he didn't have to forget about them, just keep them as a memory without letting it drag him down.

Waking up to Celina wrapped around him had felt so good at first. Then he'd realized that she wasn't his wife and guilt tore into him. After a few minutes he managed to climb out of that hole and appreciate having someone close again. Letting himself enjoy the companionship and closeness having her there had given him went a long way to reminding him that he was human and needed it to remain sane. Eight years of being alone had almost taken his sanity from him.

"As cold as it is, I think we need to forgo bathing until it warms up some. We can suck it up and deal with the body odor for a few days." Russell's voice held humor in it.

"I usually don't bathe unless I have to when it's this cold," Abe said. "Think you can handle the stench, Celina?"

She chuckled. "If you can handle mine, I can handle yours. If it gets too bad, there are clothespins in the pantry we can use."

Russell laughed along with Celina. Abe could feel the beginnings of a smile curve his lips. He relaxed against the chair once again and closed his eyes. It felt good to have others to share the hardships with. He hadn't realized how much he'd missed it until first Russell then Celina showed up. Yeah, the added responsibility was difficult to accept at times, but he thought that maybe the benefits outweighed the pitfalls.

"I'm really kind of tired. Do you guys mind if I go ahead and go to bed?" Celina asked.

Abe opened his eyes. With the mattress between the fireplace and the couch and chairs, she was probably colder sitting there than she would be in bed. He should have thought of that and suggested she go ahead and get in bed earlier.

"Of course not," Russell answered before he did.

"Um, I need to change into my pj's. Would you mind, um turning your backs for a minute?"

Abe could hear the uncertainty in her voice. He stood up and nodded toward the kitchen at Russell.

"We'll wait in the kitchen for you."

Without a word, Russell followed him into the other room. He didn't miss the soft sigh of relief from Celina as he passed the couch. He guessed that though it had only been a couple of days, she was still uncomfortable around them to some extent. That was to be expected considering she was a rare commodity to some men.

"She told me you took her coffee privileges away from her." Russell grinned at him.

"Coffee's not good for the baby. You should know that. You've had kids."

Russell's eyes dimmed some. "Yeah. I just didn't think about it to say anything. She was pouting about it."

"She'll get past it. We need to make sure she stays as warm as possible. I'm going to look through the mess upstairs to find some thermals that might fit her."

"Good idea. I'm sure there are other things we need to be thinking about concerning her pregnancy. Too bad we don't have a book on it." Russell ran a hand over his face.

"Hadn't thought about that. There's a bunch of survivalist books in the office. There might be something in there. You look through the books for one in the morning. I guess if we're going to be birthing a baby, we need to get ready."

Russell smiled once again. "Going to be different having a baby around here. You went from recluse to a full-fledged family almost at one time."

"This isn't a family. It's just a bunch of people living in one place. Don't go making this into something it isn't. No doubt she wouldn't appreciate it. She's still mourning her husband."

"It was just a figure of speech. Besides, what is wrong with becoming a family anyway? We watch out for each other and help take care of each other. That's a family. Just because there's no intimacy doesn't mean we can't still care about each other."

"Russell, you take that attitude and you're going to end up fucking up. You're going to start assigning feelings to her she'll never return and that leads to pain and disappointment. Don't go there, man." Abe walked over to the door and knocked on it. "You decent out there? It's cold in here." He knew he was growling when he spoke.

"Come in. I'm sorry. I just figured you would come back." Celina's voice from the other side of the door was muffled, but it conveyed her guilt at having kept them in the cold.

Abe felt low at having instigated her anguish in the first place. They hadn't been that cold. He'd taken his annoyance from Russell's comments out on her. That wasn't fair. He needed to apologize, but he didn't know how.

Celina's concerned expression peeked up at him from where she was snuggled with the covers pulled up to her chin on the bed. He sighed before stepping to the end of the mattress and tending to the fire. It was late. He might as well go to bed, too. He was sure Russell would agree. They had another few days of the icy snow to deal with before the weather warmed up enough it would melt some.

After adding a log and assuring the screen was in front of the fire, Abe walked back around behind the couch and began shucking his clothes without a word. He wasn't worried about Celina seeing him. He had no modesty, and from her position on the mattress on the other side of the couch, she couldn't see him anyway. Russell joined him and shed his clothes as well. They left them draped over the back of the couch before hurrying to the mattress and climbing under the covers. Even with their thermals, the cold air was enough to shrivel his balls.

Celina didn't say anything and neither did he, but Russell, ever the positive one, wished them both good night. Celina answered him. Abe just grunted.

Chapter Nine

"Crap!" Celina shook her hand before hurrying over to the sink to run cold water over where she'd burned it on the stove.

"What's wrong?" Abe grabbed her wrist and pulled it toward him.

"I burned my hand getting the biscuits out. It's fine. Just a little one."

"We don't have medicine. Nothing is minor, Celina." He looked closely at the small blister that had formed on the heel of her right hand.

"It's not too bad, Abe. I'll be careful with it. It will heal in no time." She tried to pull her hand from his grasp.

"Be still." His rumbly voice stopped her from trying to remove her hand from his grasp.

While he looked it over, she watched his face. Usually devoid of expression, there was one of intense worry now. It startled her. They had all been living together for almost three weeks now and this was the first time she'd really noticed him showing anything other than a blank expression or anger. It was hard to look away from the beauty of his face with emotion in it. Warmth flooded her body at the feel of his hand on her skin.

"I think it will be okay, but try not to break the blister. Don't wash the dishes. We'll take care of them." He looked up and caught her staring at him and not her hand. "What?"

"Nothing." She looked away. "I'll be careful."

He seemed to suddenly realize he was still holding her hand and let it go. Taking a step back, she tried to reign in the blast of heat that traveled over her body. Awareness of him as a man tickled her senses, making her uncomfortable with where her thoughts were taking her. She took another step back.

"Um, the food will be ready in about ten minutes. Would you tell Russell?" she asked turning away from him.

Celina was sure her face had turned red by the heat she could feel in her cheeks. What was going on with her? She hadn't felt this flustered around a man since her husband. Lately, being around either Abe or Russell seemed to stir her up, and that wasn't a good thing. She was pregnant, for goodness' sake.

The sound of the kitchen door swinging shut let her know that Abe had left the room. She instantly felt a sense of loss. The man had a commanding presence as well as the fact he seemed to fill a room with his huge body. She often felt as if he sucked all of the oxygen out of the room when he was in it.

Fanning her face, Celina hurried to finish preparing the meal. They were bound to be hungry after working all morning. Even with a good bit of the snow gone, the resulting slush and mud made walking outside almost dangerous. One or the other of them had shown up several times in the last few days covered in mud and cursing a blue streak after having fallen in the mess. She knew they were miserable, and the threat of catching their death of pneumonia scared her. She didn't know what they would do if that happened. With no medicine, getting sick in any way was almost a certain death sentence.

"Hey, sweetness. Something smells wonderful in here." Russell walked over to where the stew was bubbling on the stove.

"Have a seat, and I'll bring it to the table." She picked up the pot holders and tried to move him out of the way.

"Naw, it's too heavy for you. I'll get it." He reached for the pot holders.

Celina reluctantly gave them up, even though she knew she could handle the pot. If it made Russell feel good to help, she would give in. He was always so sweet to her and tended to tease her mercilessly. Sometimes she wasn't so sure it was mere teasing for him. He would get this look in his eyes that made her think he wasn't playing around, but then it would be gone and she would tell herself she'd imagined it. That look was happening more and more often, though.

"Thanks, Russell. There's already a place on the table for it. Is Abe coming?"

"Yeah, he's on his way."

She followed Russell with the plate of biscuits and a bowl of rice. She had planned for them to spoon the stew over the rice. She hoped there was enough. She was still trying to get used to feeding two men with as big of appetites as they seemed to have. Roger had never eaten as much as these two men could put away.

As soon as Abe appeared, they settled down to eat. The men talked about the weather and their chores while she watched them. What was so different about them that she couldn't stop looking at them? It bothered her that she couldn't put her finger on whatever it was that drew her to them like a moth to a flame. All she thought about when they were outside was if they were okay and when they were inside, she could barely manage to stay away from them.

Even though the weather wasn't as bitterly cold as it had been, they were still sleeping on the mattress in front of the fire. Every evening she almost held her breath that they would decide they didn't need to continue sleeping together. She'd gotten used to being between them, and the thought of going back to sleep in her bed all alone started an ache inside of her. She felt safer between them and if she were being honest with herself, she enjoyed the tiny bit of intimacy it gave her.

"How is your hand feeling?"

Celina all but jumped out of her chair at the gruff sound of Abe's voice. She dropped her hand from where it had risen to cover her heart.

"It's fine." She held her palm up to show him.

"You were a thousand miles away over there. What were you thinking so hard about?" Russell's wry grin told her he had his suspicions.

Celina didn't want either man to know how much she had come to care about them and depend on them. While Russell would probably only tease her about it, she was sure Abe wouldn't appreciate her attentions.

"Nothing really. I guess I was just thinking about what spring would be like here. I've never really been this far west or north before."

"Work. That's what it's going to be like. Lots of work." Abe got up and gathered some of the dishes.

Russell winked at her. "Bet the trees will be pretty as they bud out and the grass will probably be an amazing shade of green in the pasture."

"Stop painting some kind of pretty picture for her and help me with these dishes." Abe all but growled from across the kitchen.

She stood up and started to pick up her dishes as well. Russell stopped her and took them away from her with a broad grin.

"Go relax for a while. You probably need to put your feet up. You've been on them all morning."

"But you're the ones who've been outside in the cold, working. I don't feel comfortable sitting around while you do my dishes."

Russell opened his mouth to answer her, but Abe beat him to it.

"Don't be ridiculous. I used to do all of it by myself. The two of us can handle a few dishes. Do what Russell said and put your feet up."

Celina bit her lips but hurried into the other room. Truthfully she was grateful for a few minutes alone before they joined her. She needed to get control of herself. Just the sound of Abe's deep voice had her juices flowing. The way Russell looked at her sent heat searing through her bloodstream. It had to be the pregnancy hormones. It was the only thing she could think of. Surely she wouldn't be this attracted to two near strangers like this.

As she relaxed on the couch with her feet warm under a blanket, scenes from the last few days played over and over in her mind. Again and again, evidence of just how much they affected her played out to mock her. By the time the men walked in, Celina had come to realize that she was quickly falling under their spell. Not love, but most definitely lust. The only thing she could do now was figure out what she was going to do about it, because there was no ignoring the low burning that was slowly making its way through her body.

* * * *

Russell knew he was pushing Celina, but he couldn't help himself. There was something about her that was thawing the cold shell that had encased his heart since losing his wife. He wasn't dumb enough to believe that she would return his feelings, but he knew she wouldn't throw a little honest caring back in his face. She needed it now more than ever with a child on the way.

He gently lifted her feet off the couch and sat down before easing them back onto his lap. Her soft smile brightened the room. Russell slipped his hands beneath the cover and massaged first one and then the other of her tiny feet.

"Mmm. That feels so good."

Abe's frown and disapproving glare didn't stop him for even a second. The other man needed to relax and go easy around the pretty little female. She needed softness and gentle touches, not gruff words and hard looks.

Russell sighed and continued caressing her feet. Maybe she would enjoy a full back rub later. He was sure that as the baby grew and moved around in her body that she had new aches and pains she'd never had before. He could remember... Russell cut those thoughts off. Remembering would do no good. He wanted to concentrate on

Celina and being friends. Maybe over time, they could become closer than friends. All he knew was that her laughter made him happy.

"Are her feet swollen?" Abe asked.

Russell looked over to where the other man was standing to the side of the fireplace, watching them. The guarded gaze didn't fool Russell. He could tell the other man did feel something for Celina.

"Maybe a little bit. Not much, though. It's still early in her pregnancy yet to worry too much about that."

"Worry about what?"

Russell winced. He hadn't wanted her to worry about anything. He would do the worrying for her.

"Sometimes during pregnancy if your feet and ankles swell a lot it can be a sign of high blood pressure. You don't need to worry about that right now. Just make sure you continue to drink plenty of water and rest when you're tired. Leave the rest to us."

He watched as she looked from him to Abe and back. "Why would you worry about me? You've got enough to worry about with all of the work outside."

"You're having a baby, woman. That means the closer you get to your time, the more we're going to have to watch out for you. Your job is to take care of yourself so we can concentrate on the rest." Abe's rough voice did little to soften his harsh words. "I'm going back out to deal with the horses."

"I'll be out in a few minutes." Russell ground his teeth, annoyed at his friend's lack of sensitivity.

He heard her soft sigh and knew she felt like a problem they had to deal with. That wasn't the truth. She wasn't a problem to him. She was a gift amid the horrible life they'd had to endure. All he could think when he was around her was how precious she was and that he would do whatever it took to keep her safe and make her happy.

With that thought, he stood up and stepped toward the other end of the couch, where she sat propped against the arm. He urged her with one hand to sit up, and he scooted her into his lap as he took her place. Resting his cheek against her temple, Russell let the warmth from her body seep deeper into the coldness that had lived in his heart for the last year.

"You feel wonderful, Celina. I could sit here holding you all day."

"I imagine that wouldn't win you any points with Abe, though," she said with a chuckle.

He could feel her laughter vibrate across his skin. The welcome feeling soon had his cock hardening beneath her. He wanted to curse his body's reaction since it meant he needed to get up before she noticed it. The fact of the matter was that he was to know he could still get hard after his wife's death. For so long guilt over having been such an arrogant ass, thinking he didn't need help to keep her safe, had kept him from feeling any sort of arousal.

"I'm sure you're right, but I'm going to hold you for a few more minutes. I like holding you."

"I like it when you hold me. I like it when you smile at me, too."

Russell watched as she looked away when she said that. Hope took root in his heart that maybe she really did feel something for him more than just caring for another human being in a bad situation.

"Good. I plan to hold you and smile at you every chance I get." He squeezed her lightly before kissing her temple.

Her soft intake of breath told him she'd felt his kiss. He hadn't really meant to do it, but now that he had, Russell wasn't going to apologize for it.

After several more minutes, he knew he was pushing his luck. They really did have a lot to do outside. He needed to get up and help Abe. Standing up, he turned and carefully settled Celina back on the couch, drawing the blanket closer around her.

"Rest for a while longer before you get up to do anything else. I'll see you later, Celina."

"Be careful out there, Russell." She smiled up at him.

He had to fight to keep from pulling her back into his arms and kissing her breathless. Instead, he nodded and turned away to stalk over to the door where his coat, hat, gloves, and boots were.

Making sure to close the door firmly behind him, Russell strode across the packed snow to the check the cow's water trough to be sure ice hadn't formed over it again. It wasn't long before he was lost in thought as he worked. He didn't even hear Abe walk up until the big man had grabbed his arm.

"Fuck!" Russell jerked back before he caught himself.

"You need to stop daydreaming about the female and stay aware of everything around you or you're going to end up getting hurt."

"You can't look me in the eyes and tell me you haven't been thinking about her, too. I've seen the look on your face when you watch her." Russell glared at his friend.

"I'd have to be blind *not* to be aware of her when she's under my nose every day."

"She deserves to be treated better than you treat her, Abe. She's pregnant and living with two strange men. You need to let her get to know you better."

Abe cursed under his breath before he spoke again. "She's a new widow, Russell. If you want to get mixed up in her hormones, fine. Just don't say I didn't warn you to steer clear of that mess."

"I don't get you. We're living in the back of hell, surviving from hand to mouth with no guarantee that the next snow storm won't kill us or the next harvest will be enough to feed us through winter, and you're not willing to share something of yourself with a fellow human being. Are you really that cold, Abe? She needs comfort and support right now."

"So you're not looking to warm her bed in the process of being friendly?" Abe asked with a smirk.

Russell ground his teeth in anger. He wasn't going to start a fight with him. The man had been alone for eight years. He evidently didn't

know how to reach out anymore. Russell refused to believe that he
didn't long for more somewhere deep down inside.

"I care about her. If something more comes of it, then great. If not,
then it just doesn't. It won't change the fact that she's my friend and
that I will look out for her and her child. Basic human warmth and
understanding goes a long way to filling some of the empty places in
a man's heart, Abe. I know how you feel. I lost my family, too.
Nothing will ever replace them for me, but sometimes there's room
enough to allow someone else inside."

Russell shook his head before he turned away from the man
staring at him with such a cynical and dismal expression marring his
face. If he hadn't known Abe's history, he might have mistaken the
man's bleak outlook as his just being an asshole, but Russell knew
that his friend had suffered just as much as he had. He was thankful
every day for that bear that had nearly killed him. Had the attack not
happened, he might never have met Abe and seen firsthand what
years of total isolation could do to a man. He refused to become like
his friend. Now all he had to do was figure out how to pull Abe back
from the pervasive abyss he'd gotten sucked into before it was too
late.

Chapter Ten

Abe watched his friend go. Disgust at what he'd said to Russell rested bitter in his throat. Why had he asked something crude like that in the first place? He could see that Russell really cared about Celina. He wasn't the type of man to jump into bed with someone just for the hell of it. Russell had a strong sense of right and wrong as well as a great deal of respect for Celina.

Had he really sunk so low that he would lash out at his only friend and speak harshly of a helpless female all alone and pregnant? He should be happy that Russell and Celina could find some measure of comfort with each other. They deserved to smile and enjoy what little life had to offer them in their desolate world. It was obvious that Abe had been alone too long. He had lost the ability and skills necessary to be a good friend. Where did that leave him now?

"Hell." Standing around wasn't getting the rest of the chores done.

He carefully picked his way toward the wood pile to add logs to the dwindling stack on the porch. With them all sleeping together in front of the fire at night, they hadn't used quite as much wood as if they'd tried to keep the entire cabin warm during the night. If he were truthful with himself, he'd admit that they really didn't need to continue sleeping downstairs now that the bitter cold had passed. Instead of admitting that he liked sleeping with Celina and waking up to her wrapped around him the next morning, Abe reasoned that they would only have to move the mattress down again when the next arctic blast dipped down to blanket them in frigid temperatures once again.

He didn't know what excuses he would dream up as the weather warmed up in the spring. Maybe by then he would have gotten her out of his system. If Russell looked deeper, he would know the truth of Abe's gruffness around Celina. He did care about her, too much, and it scared him.

As he carried the last load of wood to the porch, Russell joined him. Neither man spoke until Abe had unloaded the logs onto the pile. He straightened and wiped the back of his sleeve across his brow.

"Does it bother you that she's carrying another man's son, Abe? Is that what keeps you from being a little more friendly toward her?" Russell asked before he opened the door to go inside.

Abe grabbed the other man's arm and stopped him from turning the knob.

"Her being pregnant has nothing to do with anything outside of figuring out how to keep them both safe." He struggled to get his thoughts straight before he opened his mouth again. "Losing my family nearly drove me crazy. They were my everything. To care about someone even half that much and then lose them as well would more than devastate me. I'm not sure I'm strong enough to take that chance."

"There are two of us, Abe. We can keep her and the child safe together."

"But what if in a few months or even a few years she decides that she made a mistake and doesn't want one or both of us anymore? She just lost her husband, Russell. How can she possibly be thinking clearly right now with everything that she has going on with her?"

"Maybe she isn't, I don't know. What I do know is that I care about her and want her to be healthy and happy. The way she's living right now isn't working. She's not gaining weight and she's exhausted even when she first wakes up. She needs to feel wanted and safe. I want to make sure she has everything she needs to feel those things."

Abe ran his hand around the back of his neck in an effort to relieve some of the tension that was building there. He knew Russell was right. He'd noticed that Celina hadn't gained any weight and that she had dark circles under her eyes. Guilt slithered around like a snake in his soul.

"I care about her a lot, Russell. I don't know, maybe I even love her. There's something about her that draws me no matter how hard I try to keep my distance. Sometimes I want to bury myself inside of her so deep she never forgets who I am, but then I worry that it's too soon for her."

"Maybe it would have been before the world changed, but I don't think it is now. We have no guarantees that we'll live beyond this night. I loved my wife more than anything. I will always love her, but there's room in my heart for Celina as well. She fills me with happiness and gives me a reason to love again. I want to be part of her life and share raising her child." Russell had let go of the door knob and was watching him.

"What makes you think she would accept both of us?" Abe finally asked.

"She watches you when you're not looking. I think she is attracted to you but is afraid you would reject her."

"I don't want her to be afraid of me." Abe snorted.

"She's not afraid of *you*, Abe. She's afraid of rejection. I think if you would touch her more and talk to her, she would relax around you," Russell said.

"You're right. I'll try to temper my attitude around her and be more supportive. It's been a long time, Russell. My social skills are a bit rusty."

The other man chuckled. "You could say that."

"I want to hold her, Russell. Do you think she would let me?"

"I think that we need to show her that we desire her and want her as a woman, as *our* woman."

"How do we go about doing that without freaking her out?" Abe asked in a gruff voice.

"Let's not wear shirts to bed tonight. We can keep her warm between us using our body heat while getting her used to our bodies. I'm thinking that she wants what we want but is just as nervous about showing it as we are."

"Okay. I'll follow your lead, but I don't want her to feel coerced or pressured into being with us if she doesn't really want to."

Russell smiled and nodded. "I agree, but I don't think we have anything to worry about."

Abe clasped him on the shoulder then shoved him forward into the warmth of the cabin. Immediately the smell of warm bread and something spicy enveloped him in a welcoming cocoon of comfort. It hit him square in the heart that it smelled like home to him now. And that was what he'd been afraid would happen all along if he let down his guard. It looked like it hadn't mattered after all. He was lost and not even sure if he cared anymore.

* * * *

Celina could almost touch the pulsing tension that hung in the air as they prepared for bed. Both of the men seemed to be watching her all during dinner. Then when she started to gather up the dishes, Abe had startled her when he picked her up and carried her into the great room where he set her on the couch to *rest* while they took care of the dishes. Since he had hardly voluntarily touched her before, it had scared her at first.

She quickly slipped beneath the covers as the two men peeled out of their clothes until all they were wearing was the bottoms to their thermal underwear. Normally they wore the tops as well. When they climbed in on either side of her, she shivered, and she wasn't so sure it was from the cooler air that trickled in with them. The realization that she would be able to touch all of the bare flesh that covered hard muscles stopped her breath from leaving her lungs.

She froze as they settled under the covers beside her. She longed to snuggle between them, skin to delicious skin, but couldn't make the first move. Before the thought had completely left her mind, both men moved closer until they were pressed tightly against her sides. A slight gasp escaped her lips at the heat their hard bodies produced.

"Easy, Celina." Abe's deep voice jerked her attention to him.

Celina couldn't control the fine tremors that traveled down her body. Being this close to them without the added barrier of their shirts sped her heartbeat up until she was sure it would gallop out of her chest. She had longed for them for night after endless night and now that she was experiencing it, she wasn't sure how to survive it. Their hot bodies elicited more than feelings of comfort and safety. They sparked naughty thoughts of illicit sex and long hours of uninhibited exploration into what shouldn't be.

She couldn't stop her mind from exploring the endless possibilities of being with both men, but both guilt and propriety waged an internal war within her heart. Yes, she cared about both of them. Yes, she might easily fall in love with them, but was it right?

They were two strong men who could easily keep her and her baby safe. They would provide for her and her child regardless of a sexual relationship between them or not. There was no doubt in her mind of that, but why deny all of them the pleasure that they could have if she accepted them as her lovers? Did wanting both of them make her a loose woman? Confusion filled her head as she tried to make sense of it all.

The first touch of a hand on her hip sent sparks straight to her pussy. The seemingly innocent touch had her wet in less than a second. When another hand touched her upper arm, she gasped as tiny sparkles of electricity shot across to her breasts. Instantly her nipples hardened beneath the cotton pajama top that covered them.

"Celina?" Russell's voice snapped her eyes in his direction.

Outlined by the fire, she could barely make out his face. The expression, though shadowed, appeared worried. Did he not feel the same things she was experiencing? That thought caused a sinking feeling in her stomach. If she were the only one having these hot delicious feelings, it would be worse than devastating. It would humiliate her to know that they didn't see her as a desirable woman.

"Celina?" He spoke again. "What's wrong? You're shaking."

"I–I…" She couldn't finish the sentence.

"She's nervous with us not wearing shirts. I was right, Russell. She isn't interested in us like that." Abe's body tensed beside her before leaving one side of her suddenly bare to the cold.

"Is that true, sweetness? Do you want us to leave you alone?" Russell asked.

His mouth hovered just above her ear. The wet heat of his breath there sent another wave of chills coursing through her body. She couldn't think, but one thought did manage to break through. She didn't want them leaving her alone. She needed their touch, needed to know that they were there. Her body craved their touch, and if she was honest with herself, her heart needed them as well.

"Please. Don't go." Her voice sounded weak and breathy.

The next thing she knew, Abe's big, strong hand cupped her chin and turned her head toward him. Even in the dim light, Celina could see the vulnerable need in his dark eyes. He had never allowed her to see anything like this before. She recognized the gift bestowed in his eyes and accepted it for what it was—a miracle.

As his head slowly lowered until his lips touched hers, she had a moment to wonder at what it all meant. Was this just for tonight, or would this be her future? Then all thoughts flew away as pure, raw arousal filled her senses when Abe's tongue licked across her lower lip. When her mouth parted in a small gasp, he took quick advantage and slipped between her lips to probe her mouth with his wicked tongue.

They slid alongside each other before he stroked it along the roof of her mouth and explored every crevice with a thoroughness that left her fighting to breathe. Even after they broke apart, Abe continued to nip and lick along her jawline before sucking in her earlobe and nipping it. The small bite of pain only heightened the pleasure that built deep in her womb.

Russell's mouth at her throat captured her attention when he licked a long, wet line down to where her pajama top allowed a peek of the cleavage between her breasts. Cool air followed his hot mouth, eliciting more shivers that did little to cool her ardor.

"Let Russell have those beautiful breasts, baby. He wants to suck on your nipples. Can he love your breasts, Celina?" Abe's thick voice caught at something inside of her that sent a rush of cream straight to her pussy.

Even as Abe asked her, Russell was unbuttoning her top. She had no time to protest as suddenly she was open to him. The feel of his hands on her heated, sensitive breasts heated her blood to the boiling point. As if knowing that her nipples were sensitive with her pregnancy, he gently licked and sucked the hard nubs while carefully mounding the heavy orbs.

"Fuck! That is so hot. Seeing his mouth on your breasts has my cock hard enough to pound nails." Abe's dark voice whispered into her ear. "I can't wait to sink my dick deep inside your hot cunt."

"Oh, God! What are you doing to me?"

"Loving you, sweetness. Giving you what you deserve. Open up and let us pleasure you." Russell sounded as if he were just this side of pain.

His mouth moved from one nipple to the other and then he licked a decadent path down her body as he rid her of her bottoms until he rested between her naked and trembling thighs. His heated breath wisped against her pussy lips.

"Oh, hell, you smell so damn good, Celina. I want to suck every last drop of your sweet honey," Russell said.

She wanted him to, wanted to feel his tongue on her clit, making her come. It took all of her control to keep from grinding her pussy against him. All she wanted to do was roll her body all over these two men until their dark, rich scents covered her body. Never had she felt so primal. Was it because of her pregnancy? Was it just hormones, or did she truly want them like a woman wanted a man?

The first swipe of Russell's tongue across her pussy was pure heaven. Then he used the tip of the talented organ to delve between her folds and stab deep into her cunt. His low growl when she gushed her juices only released more. He lapped at her as if he couldn't get enough. Then she felt Abe move quickly down her body and push Russell out of the way.

"My turn. I can smell her cunt from here. It's driving me crazy."

Russell didn't seem to mind too much as he crawled up her body and shared her taste when he kissed her slow and deep. It awakened even more needs deep inside of her that she'd thought either no longer existed or were dead. In that instant, Celina realized that it wasn't true. Her needs, her body was very much alive.

Her body was burning up now. Even bare to the world and nothing covering her but the warm bodies of her lovers, Celina was no longer cold in the least. Her shivers were of pure desire and the realization that these two sexy men were actually interested in her. She had a rather rounded belly that actually poked out in front of her. What could they possibly see in her?

Dark thoughts that they didn't really see anything in her at all but were just looking for a fuck all but blindsided her. Instantly her need slipped away and her body cooled. The men seemed to notice, and immediately they pulled back to stare down into her eyes.

"What is it, Celina?" Russell peered deep into her eyes.

She stared up into his, searching for the truth of what he wanted. Then she gazed into Abe's from where he leaned on his hands above her, his body still intimately cradled between her thighs.

"What's going on, baby?" he asked.

"Why are you doing this now?"

"We've been fighting this for weeks. You had just lost your husband and were trying to learn to trust two complete strangers. It just didn't seem like the right time." Russell's eyes seemed to be pleading with her to understand.

"What has changed?" she asked in a husky voice, tight with tears.

"You've been more open to us and seemed to respond when we touched you. But if this isn't what you want, we'll back off." Russell didn't move away from her or appear to have any plans to. Neither did Abe, for that matter.

"I want you both, but I'm scared." She looked first at Abe and then at Russell.

Did either of them truly care? Was she just a vessel for them to slack their lust? Somehow that hurt even more than she would have believed possible. She knew it wasn't that way for her. She truly cared about them and craved their attention. Maybe it wasn't love, but it was more than just a sexual itch she wanted scratched, wasn't it? Now she doubted her own reasoning. She started to pull back, but Abe appeared to have decided that action was what was needed. He plunged two fingers deep inside of her cunt and sucked her clit between his teeth.

She couldn't have stopped the scream if she had wanted to. His name left her lips in a rush of air that she was sure had reached all the way to the river. Abe teased her mercilessly with his tongue before finally drawing fully on it until an orgasm slammed her full force, causing her to arch off the mattress.

"Damn she's beautiful, Abe." Russell's voice pierced the ringing in her ears as she settled down once again.

No sooner had she caught her breath before Abe had her on all fours with his thick cock at her entrance, teasing her pussy lips. She tried to press back against him, but he held her firmly in place.

"Suck Russell's cock, baby. He needs to come, too. Make him feel good with that hot mouth of yours."

She opened her mouth as soon as the mushroom cockhead of Russell's dick brushed her lips. Gentle hands held her head as he slowly fed the hardened shaft to her.

"Ah, yes. That feels so fucking amazing. Your mouth feels like wet silk around my dick."

Celina hummed in satisfaction as he slowly rocked in and out rubbing her lips over his sensitive skin. Occasionally, she let her teeth graze him, enjoying the sharp hiss it caused.

Then Abe stole her breath and her attention by plunging his cock deep into her cunt. Her pussy's muscles quivered around him as he held still while she stretched to accommodate him. His cock was much larger than anything she'd even played with before. With her late husband being the only man she'd ever been with, Abe's wide girth was a shock to her system.

"You are so damn tight, baby. I'm not going to be able to last long this time. It's been so long and you feel amazing." Abe's thick voice had gone so low and soft, she had a hard time hearing him.

"Please don't stop, Abe. I'll die if you stop now." She hated begging, but her body was on fire again, and she didn't think anything could put it out but him.

"You take care of Russell, Celina. I'll take care of you." A sharp slap fell on her ass cheek, startling her.

Russell's strained laugh in front of her made her smile just before he filled her mouth once again. She ran her tongue up and around his dick in a swirling motion before sucking her way back up his shaft. His fingers flexed against her scalp. Though he held her head in a light grip, he didn't force her down on him or ram his hard cock down her throat. It helped her to relax and accept his light thrusts so much easier.

Abe's retreat and quick return thrust deep inside her pussy had her moaning around Russell, which soon had him cursing above her.

"Whatever you're doing, man, don't stop. The vibrations from her moaning are driving me insane. I'm never going to last long like this. Hell. I don't even want to last long. This feels too fucking good to last."

The other man didn't waste a breath responding. He gripped her hips in his big hands and shuttled his long shaft in and out of her hot, wet cunt with measured strokes that were driving her to distraction. She wanted more, faster, harder. With Russell's cock in her mouth, she could only whimper and try to push back against the mountain of a man behind her. He gave her no room to maneuver, though. She was totally and completely at his mercy.

"Russell?" Abe's strained voice seemed to be saying something more than the other man's name.

"Can't—stop it."

Suddenly Abe reached around and began stroke her clit with one finger. The callused pad of his finger rubbed her just the right way, and within seconds, her orgasm had her screaming around Russell's hard dick while Abe pounded her pussy with his wide cock. She felt Russell's release pulse in her throat even as her climax squeezed Abe's from him. She could feel hot ribbons of cum fill her womb as Russell pulled from her mouth. She collapsed to the bed with her ass in the air, thanks to Abe's hands holding it there against him as he shuttered over her.

Celina shivered at the shock of cold air that snuck beneath the covers as one of the men left their bed, but she couldn't seem to make her eyelids cooperate to figure out which one it was. Then another tendril of cold air roused her once again as he returned. A warm, wet cloth wiped her face then proceeded to clean between her legs. She only offered a token effort at resistance, because she had no energy left to complain.

The last thing she remembered was how good it felt to be nearly crushed between two hard bodies and that she hoped it never ended.

Chapter Eleven

The next morning, Celina woke before the men. She suddenly felt nervous and shy around them. She didn't know what to think, having never had the experience of a morning after before. She'd been a virgin when she and her husband had gotten married. This was new to her.

No sooner had she started easing from beneath the covers than an arm encircled her waist and anchored her to the mattress.

"Where are you going?" Abe asked, his voice husky.

"To get dressed and start the coffee." Her voice squeaked.

"Hmmm, not yet. You feel too good to let go of."

Abe, still caught in the last vestiges of sleep, was always a little possessive in wanting to hold her. She couldn't help but wonder if anything had changed between them after last night.

Russell moved on the other side of her, and his hard cock pressed against her thigh. She couldn't stop the instant ache that erupted in her body. She was sure her pussy was wet with her juices. Abe's thick dick rubbed suggestively between her ass cheeks. Things had defiantly changed.

"Are you too sore, sweetness?" Russell asked as he kissed her neck.

"No." She wanted to add that she wanted them, too, but couldn't quite make the words leave her mouth.

"Good. I think a sleep-in is in order this morning." Russell nipped at her shoulder before pulling one leg up over his hip and fitting his pulsing cock to her entrance. "Hold on to Abe's neck. I'm going to take you for a ride, Celina."

It was all the warning she got before he plunged into her wet pussy. She gasped as he slowly pulled almost all the way out and entered her again. His hard dick filled her cunt, rubbing against tissues that came alive as he thrust in and out of her over and over.

She gripped Abe's neck behind her as he continued to rub his hard cock between her ass cheeks. The added sensation helped build the pressure inside of her to come. Russell shifted and the new angle seemed to open her even more for both men. Even as he gripped her hip and thigh, holding her in place, Abe cupped her breasts, running his fingers over her aching nipples.

"Please!" she gasped.

"What, baby? What do you need?" Abe asked.

"I don't know," she sobbed. "More. I need more."

Russell increased his thrusts so that without Abe's solid body to hold her still, Celina had no doubt she would have slid across the bed. Abe pinched and pulled on her nipples until lights exploded behind her eyes as she succumbed to a mind blowing orgasm that left her panting and seeing stars.

She had barely settled down before Abe took Russell's place when he pulled out by entering her from behind. Before she had taken another breath, she was on her knees with her ass lifted in the air. Abe's big hands held her steady as he thrust his thick dick deep into her still-spasming cunt. In no time, her body began to tighten as another orgasm built deep inside of her. She couldn't believe she could possibly climax again so soon after the first one.

"Fuck, you are so tight. I'm not going to last. Russell. Help her." Abe's deep voice sounded strained beyond measure.

Russell reached beneath her and brushed his finger over her clit in light touches. He sought out her mouth with his own and kissed her, his lips crushing hers then pulling her lower one inside his mouth. He sucked on it in rhythm to his finger rubbing against her throbbing clit. An orgasm erupted from somewhere deep within her, splintering her into tiny pieces. Abe followed her over with a hoarse shout then put her back together with a single kiss on her shoulder and a whispered *thank you.*

Both men petted and rubbed her as she caught her breath trying not to slip back into sleep. She could feel her heart stretching already. They were going to make a home there. She had no doubt that before long, she was going to be totally in love with these two men, for better or for worse.

"We'll see to the coffee and starting breakfast this morning, baby. You go get a nice, hot shower and dress warmly. You need some fresh air, and today is going to be a nice one for a short walk." Abe popped her ass lightly before shoving the covers down and letting the chilly morning air motivate her into action.

Nearly thirty minutes later, Celina strode into the kitchen, freshly showered and feeling lighter than she had in a long time. She was sure her face would break apart from the wide smile that rested there. She found the men frying eggs and buttering bread for toast.

"Have a seat, Celina. Breakfast is almost ready." Russell set a glass of milk on the table in front of her.

"Couldn't I have just a sip of coffee every morning?" she asked in hopes their good mood would extend to allowing her coffee.

"Not going to happen, babe. No coffee for you." Abe chuckled at her pout.

"You keep that up and we might change our minds about going for that walk later," Russell teased.

Celina sighed and sipped at the milk. She still, after all these years, hadn't quite gotten used to the way fresh milk tasted. The richness was almost too much for her palate.

After breakfast, once all the dishes had been washed and put away, the men helped her bundle up to go outside. By the time they were satisfied she wouldn't get cold, Celina wasn't so sure she could walk through the door, much less go for a short walk. They'd piled the layers on until she felt like lifting her hand to scratch her nose was a near impossible feat.

"If I were to slip and fall, guys, I'll bounce away."

"That's part of the plan. We don't want you to fall at all, but if you do, maybe you won't hurt yourself or the baby. Plus, the added layers will keep you warm and dry until we get you back home." Russell adjusted the hood on her coat.

She grumbled as they led her outside into the late morning sun. It felt wonderful to feel its rays on her face when she leaned her head back. The smell of the wood smoke coming from their chimney added to the magical feel of being outside again. It had seemed like years instead of months since she'd first arrived there. Soon it would be early spring.

Despite the bright sun shining through the trees, it was still quite cold out there, and her breath fogged in the air. She followed Abe as he led them on a short walk around the compound with Russell trailing behind her. She felt very safe with them and was thankful the good Lord had led her to them.

Even though most of the snow was gone, her growing belly had her center of gravity off, and she had to concentrate to walk through the occasional snow drift. The brief excursion was invigorating as they wound up in front of the lodge once again. Even though the cold air made it almost hurt to breathe in, it felt amazing and she was sure it had helped clear her head of all the cobwebs from the last few weeks.

"Time to go inside now." Abe checked the door before he opened it and ushered them back inside.

"What were you doing to the door?" she asked once Russell had the door closed and locked behind them.

"Making sure no one had been here or was waiting inside to surprise us." Abe helped her pull off her boots with a soft grunt.

"How do you do that?"

"I put a single string across the doorway so that the wind won't blow it away, but opening the door will dislodge it and give away that someone has been or is still inside waiting."

"Wow. That's smart. I never would have thought of something like that. Have you ever had anyone show up here before?"

"Only the two of you in the eight years I've been here. I've found evidence of others walking nearby, but no one has ever actually walked into this compound before," Abe said.

She relaxed a little more and helped the two men hang up all the outerwear to dry. Then she scrambled closer to the fire. Despite having felt like a walking clothing store, Celina had gotten cold. She moved aside only long enough for Russell to tend the fire before reclaiming her spot directly in front of it. Abe walked over and held out his hands to warm them before heading toward the kitchen.

"He's going to fix coffee. Then when he finishes a cup, he'll come out here to keep me occupied while you go have a cup. You're not fooling me, Russell." She narrowed her eyes at the other man.

Russell winced. "We just hate drinking it in front of you when you can't have any."

"I'd rather you drink it in front of me instead of hiding it from me. I don't like to be lied to, about anything. Hiding something is the same thing as lying, in my book."

"I'll go tell Abe. We'll both be back in just a few minutes." Russell bent and quickly kissed her cheek before strolling away.

Celina sighed and prayed that the coffee issue was all they were lying by omission about to her. She couldn't stand it if they were hiding anything more. She didn't like any sort of subterfuge. Honesty and trust were very high on her list of expectations in any type of affiliation. Even those based only on friendship as theirs was right now. She still felt as if Abe was holding something back from her. While she didn't expect them to pledge undying love to her, she did expect them to be open about their relationship. A relationship she was still a little unsure about.

* * * *

Russell quickly explained that Celina was onto them about the coffee and didn't like it. The other man grunted and shook his head.

"She's really sensitive about lying, and she associates keeping things from her with lying. We're going to have to be careful, Abe."

"Try to make things easier for her, and she grumbles about it."

Russell winced. He could already see it would fall on him to keep them two of them from fighting over little things all the time. They were both hardheaded and opinionated. He liked it that Celina would stand up for herself. Her spirit was only just emerging now that she wasn't afraid of them anymore.

"She wasn't really fussing, Abe," Russell said.

Abe didn't comment again. He took his cup and stomped into the great room. Russell followed him, carrying his own mug of the rich coffee. He nearly burst out laughing when Celina almost fell onto Abe's lap trying to sniff the other man's coffee when he sat down.

"Hey! You're going to fall and spill coffee all over us both." Abe pushed her back from his lap.

"I just wanted to smell it if I can't drink it. It smells delicious." The pout that graced her face had Russell wishing he could slip her a sip or two now and then.

"Don't even think about it, Russell. I can hear the gears turning in your head from here. It's bad for her and the baby."

Russell didn't miss the dark scowl Celina flashed at his friend. He covered his chuckle by clearing his throat then taking another quick sip.

"Can I smell your coffee, Russell?" Her innocent, wide-eyed stare warned him that she was up to no good.

Before he could answer her, Abe reached out and snagged her wrist. He pulled her closer to his recliner.

"No, you don't. If you want to smell anyone's coffee, you're going to smell mine. I know I won't let you sneak a sip. Sit on my lap." Abe had set his cup on the table next to him and helped her up on his lap.

It was obvious by her expression that this wasn't what she'd planned to happen. She had been planning to filch a sip under the pretense of getting a good whiff of the addicting aroma. Russell watched as Abe held her hands down in her lap before lifting the mug off the table and holding it up to her face where she could get a good sniff.

"Watch the steam or you'll end up with a burnt nose."

She cocked one brow at him before leaning over to take another deep breath. He set the cup back on the table and looked at her.

"Is that enough, or do you plan to sniff it until it's too cold for me to enjoy it?" Abe asked.

"You're mean! Let go of me. I want down."

He chuckled and let go of her but kept a hand near her arm while she eased off his lap. Russell knew he wasn't really fussing with her. He just had a gruff manner about him. He was pretty sure that Celina knew it, too. When she flounced over to the couch and wrapped a blanket around her with her nose in the air, he knew he had been right. She was playing along. Russell relaxed back in the recliner and let himself enjoy the rest of the afternoon.

Celina kept glancing over at Abe as he sipped his coffee and leaned back with his eyes closed. No doubt the little schemer was making plans where Abe was concerned. He wasn't sure if that would be a good idea or not, but he wasn't going to interfere unless it looked like it might get out of hand. If this was going to work between the three of them, they had to work out their differences between themselves.

"What are you up to over there, woman?" Abe finally asked.

Russell had evidently drifted off because the other man's deep voice startled him. He looked over to where Celina had obviously been sneaking around the back of the couch. She didn't look very happy at having been caught.

"Why do you think I'm up to something? I'm just going to get dinner started. We skipped lunch since we ate such a late breakfast. I'm getting hungry."

"That's good to hear. You need to eat more." Russell smiled at her.

"I know just how much coffee I left in that pot, baby. I wouldn't try it."

"Oh, you!" She stomped off into the kitchen.

Russell chuckled. "You know she's going to figure a way to get you for that."

"I'm counting on it. It will keep her thoughts off of missing the coffee so much. We get to drink it and it helps warm us up. She's missing the benefit of the extra warmth as well as having to deal with the addiction." Abe stared down into his cup.

"I'm never going to have a dull minute with you two around to watch." Russell watched as Abe stood up and stretched.

"I'm going to go ahead and shower while she's cooking. Check on her and be sure she doesn't need anything in a few minutes. Knowing her, she'll end up standing on a chair to reach something if we don't ride heard on her."

Russell watched the other man climb the stairs. There were times that he seemed almost normal around them now. He had no doubt that it was thanks to Celina's presence. Still, he was holding back some of himself and that was eventually going to cause problems. Their woman wasn't going to let either one of them hide anything. She had a vulnerable spot that demanded that they were totally honest with her. That was where that lying by omission statement came in. The thing was, he didn't think Abe believed she was serious about it when it came to his deepest thoughts. With Celina, those were probably the most important ones she was talking about.

He gazed into the dying flames, wishing he had enough guts to ask for another cup of coffee. He sighed. If she had to go without, the least he could do was cut back. He ran his hand up and down the side of the mug for several more minutes. The aroma of cooking food finally galvanized him into action.

Russell stood up, and after adding a log to the fire, he joined her in the kitchen where he caught her trying to reach a platter in the cabinet standing on her tiptoes. No doubt a chair would have been next just like Abe had predicted.

"You do know you are going to end up hurting yourself." Russell pulled the platter down for her and closed the cabinet door.

She stuck her tongue out at him and stirred the food on the stove. "If my stomach wasn't so big, I would have been able to reach it."

"You're not big yet, baby. Just wait until there's more sticking out front than what's sticking out back."

"You asshole!" She grabbed a dish towel and popped him with it.

Russell could tell she wasn't too upset by the slight smile she tried to hide as she chased him around the table.

"What in the hell is going on in here?" Abe's loud shout surprised them both.

"N–Nothing."

"Russell. I would have thought you would know better than to let her run around like that. What if she slipped and fell?" Abe asked stomping up to where Celina stood holding the dish towel.

He snatched it out of her hand and glared at them both. Russell sighed. They weren't running very fast, but Abe was right. She might have fallen, and they didn't have medical care available now.

"We weren't running very fast, Abe. I was having fun."

"I should turn you over my knee and spank your sweet ass so you'll think next time." His scowl reminded Russell of how the man had always appeared when he'd first woken up from the bear attack.

He sure didn't want him to return to that dark, miserable man he had been. If his friend thought he couldn't count on him to act responsibly, he would shoulder all of the pressure himself and gone would be the new Abe he enjoyed being around. No, they were partners in this. He needed to keep a cool head on his shoulders and stop handing over the problems for Abe to take care of. He was an adult and should be acting like one.

"Celina. Abe is right. We shouldn't have been playing around like that. It's too dangerous. We need to be thinking about you and the baby's safety more."

Abe's obvious relief that he was standing with him on the subject told Russell just how much he'd been undermining the other man's authority by trying to get him to cut Celina more slack. In the world they lived in, they had to stay vigilant and take nothing for granite anymore.

She visibly drooped in front of them, making him feel like a heel, but he wasn't going to cave. Her health and safety and that of the child she was carrying were of utmost importance.

"Dinner is almost ready. Give me another twenty minutes and I'll have it on the table." She turned from them and walked slowly back to the stove.

Russell glanced over at Abe and saw a flash of hurt cross the man's face before he stoically hid it and walked back out of the room. He wasn't without feelings. Russell had known that, but it seemed more real now that he'd seen it. Just a brief glimpse, but it reminded him that his friend had been alone for a long, long time. He was still a little skeptical that they might be able to have another chance at happiness and, just maybe, love as well.

Chapter Twelve

Several more weeks passed, and Celina figured she was getting close to her time. Though they still got the occasional snowy day, it didn't last nearly as long. Her belly had expanded to the point that she wore all of her pants under it now and wore the largest shirts she could find to cover the giant basketball that poked out.

The men had taken to rubbing her belly any time she was close by. She swore they were making wishes when they did, as if it was some kind of good-luck charm. It had shocked her that Abe seemed to enjoy feeling the baby kick. She smiled thinking back to the first time the world-class gymnast that had been clowning around inside of her for weeks kicked Abe in the belly when he'd been asleep, pressed up against her. He'd almost broken his neck trying to figure out what was going on.

The sparkle in his eyes when he'd held his hand over her belly and felt the strong kick had melted her heart. From then on out, both he and Russell touched her belly every chance they got. Russell even talked to her belly as if a little adult resided inside of her.

They had never moved the mattress back upstairs. Abe decided she didn't need to climb those stairs so much. If she wanted a shower or bath, one of them went with her. There was a half bath downstairs that she could use, and thank the good Lord for that. As her belly grew, her bladder shrank.

She stretched as much as she could before rubbing her lower back after drying the dishes from lunch. It seemed like she had no energy anymore, and her back ached all the time now. She tried to see her feet to check how her ankles were doing, but they hadn't been on her radar for months now. She would have to sit down and prop them up in order to see them now.

"You need to rest, sweetness. I can tell your back is hurting again. Abe and I will do the dishes from now on." Russell's voice always soothed her. He never sounded anxious or upset no matter what was going on.

He ushered her out of the kitchen and into the great room, where he helped her get comfortable on the couch. That lasted all of two minutes. Then the aches were back and she groaned as she tried to readjust herself.

"Let me move that pillow," Russell said.

She sat up with his help as he plumped the pillow and moved it over for her. As she leaned back with a sigh of relief, she caught sight of her bloated ankles and feet. Not good. Not good at all. She had a slight headache as well. That meant her blood pressure was probably up. If Abe saw them before they went down some, he would be upset.

She closed her eyes and willed herself to relax so that she could rest and maybe lose the headache before he came back inside. She could hear Russell moving around in the room.

"Are you thirsty, honey?"

"No, but thanks. I'm fine." She didn't open her eyes.

"I don't think you're drinking enough water, Celina."

"Russell. I'm fine. I'll drink some more in a few minutes. I'll have to get up and go to the bathroom again, and I just got comfortable." She winced when she realized she had probably spoken harshly.

"I'm leaving a glass of water on the table next to you. I'll be back inside in a few minutes to check on you again."

She nodded but didn't say anything. She was just too tired to worry about anything right then. If only her back would ease up some. She was sure being on her feet so much wasn't helping either the swelling or the throb in her back. Maybe she should relinquish one of the meals to the men. They had offered often enough. Celina was afraid of appearing too fragile and needy. If she was more trouble than she was worth, they might change their minds about wanting her around.

In all the years she and Roger had been together, she had always pulled her own weight and made sure she wasn't a burden on anyone. Her husband had never complained or said anything to worry her about it, but she could remember how some of the men would harass their women about being lazy and not working hard enough. She never wanted to hear someone say she was worthless.

Slowly the pain in her back eased and she was able to relax enough that she fell asleep to thoughts of not being good enough for Russell and Abe.

* * * *

Abe heard Russell's call over the pasture. An uneasy feeling pricked at the back of his neck as the man's voice grew louder. Abe didn't wait for the other man to draw closer. Instead he raced across the uneven ground and climbed between the fence posts just as Russell jogged to a stop in front of him. His face appeared pale but it was the fear in the other man's eyes that had his stomach churning.

"What's wrong?" Abe grabbed the other man's shoulder and shook him.

"Celina. She's unconscious, and there's blood." Russell's voice broke before he cleared his throat and started again. "I can't wake her up. I went to pick her up and carry her closer to the fire and there was blood between her legs."

"Fuck!" Abe didn't wait for more.

Together both men ran across the back and into the open area in front of the lodge before throwing open the door and racing into the great room. He only slowed up when he approached the mattress where Russell had left her covered up to her neck.

"Get a basin of hot water and all the towels and cloth scraps you can find." He didn't bother looking up to see if Russell was following his orders.

When he touched Celina's face, it was hot and dry. He pulled the covers down to her feet and began pulling her pants and underwear off. By the time Russell had reappeared with the basin of hot water and an arm load of towels, Abe had her stripped down to her skin.

"Her feet and ankles are swollen all the way up her calves. She shouldn't have been on her feet at all today. Damn, why didn't I check them?"

"She was complaining of her back aching when I made her lie down after breakfast. I tried to get her to drink something then, but she said she would later. She was tired of having to pee all the time." Russell's voice wavered.

"Get a fresh glass of cool water and try to get a little down her. Wet her lips with it if that's all you can manage."

Abe used the warm water and towels to clean away the blood and decided that she wasn't actively bleeding any more. Neither was there any evidence that the baby was coming early. At least he assumed it would be early. They really didn't have a clue how far along she was. He cursed under his breath. If she lost the baby this far along, they stood a good chance of losing her as well. She could easily bleed to death.

"She swallowed some but not a lot," Russell said.

"Keep her lips wet and try again every few minutes. We need to get more water in her somehow."

Once he was satisfied that she was as clean as he could get her, Abe covered her up and carried the water and bloody towels to the room behind the kitchen where they did laundry. He was worried to death that Celina was dying. He needed to search through some of the books in the office and see if any of them would offer an explanation of what was going on.

By the time he had returned, Russell had managed to get half of a glass of water down her. He didn't look any better than he had earlier. Worry had etched lines across the man's face. He was sure his wouldn't look much better. As he gazed down at Celina's pale face, Abe had to accept that he was a little bit in love with the woman. He had been fighting it for weeks now, but there was no use fighting it any longer.

"I'm going to look through the books we have and see if I can figure out what is going on with her and the baby. Stay with her and keep giving her water every few minutes."

"She isn't bleeding anymore now, is she?" Russell asked.

Abe watched as his partner gently stroked Celina's cheek. As much as he wanted to be the one touching her, he needed to find out what to do to take care of her first.

"No. The bleeding had stopped. Yell if you need me."

Abe hurried down the short hall and opened the door into the office they rarely used. The temperature in the room had to be close to freezing. They kept all the unused rooms closed off. Now he left the door wide open in order to be able to hear Russell if he called for him. The wooden doors in the lodge were all thick and sturdy. It would be much harder to hear the other man if he closed the door.

For the next thirty minutes, Abe flipped through books, looking for anything that would offer an explanation of what was wrong with Celina. In all the years he had lived so far away from others, he'd never once regretted the isolation, but he was regretting it now. Now they needed someone with more experience in birthing children than either he or Russell had. All of their children had been born in hospitals from wives who'd had prenatal care.

He slammed the book he had been browsing through down on the dusty desk and swallowed around the knot forming in his throat. His eyes stung from staring hard at small print in the dim light of the lantern. So far nothing he had found offered any information on what they were dealing with. He picked up the lantern and began searching the shelves once again. There was no order to the books on the shelves and stacked around on the floor and desk. If they ever had time, they needed to work on sorting them out. There was probably a good bit of useful information to be found in some of them if they could find it when they needed it.

He located two more books that offered information on pregnancy and childbirth stuck on the bottom of a stack of books gathering cobwebs on the floor. He readjusted the lantern and began searching the table of contents. After a couple of false leads, Abe finally found something that seemed plausible to him. The only problem was that it didn't sound good for Celina or the baby.

Grabbing the other book, Abe hurried out of the office, closing the door behind him. He found Russell sitting next to Celina, holding her hand in his. He looked up with a hopeful expression.

"Did you find something?"

"I might have. It's not good, though. She could be having something called eclampsia or preeclampsia. I'm not real clear on all of it yet. I brought the books in here so we could both read on it where there was more light and it wasn't so fucking cold."

Russell took one of the books from him and settled it in his lap. While he began to read, Abe located the same subject in the book he'd kept and sat on the other side of Celina to read. The more he read, the more he was sure she might be having some of the symptoms. Her swollen ankles and moody behavior of the last few days pointed to preeclampsia, which could lead to toxemia and seizures and death.

"Damn. What are we going to do, Abe? We don't have any medicine to give her and we can't do a C-section like they say in the book."

"I know. I'm hoping that we're wrong about it being this bad. I'm going to keep looking in this book."

"Abe. I love her. I can't lose her, too."

Russell's voice held so much pain that Abe felt as if he would break down with the other man. His own feelings were too close to the surface to be able to hold it together if his friend crumbled.

"I know. She's strong and she's a stubborn woman. We're not giving up on her. How much of the water have you managed to get into her?"

"Almost the entire glass, but it's taken almost two hours now."

"I'm here. Why don't you go start some soup for us to eat in here with her and then bring another glass of water? I'll try and get some into her while you're working on the soup. I have a feeling it's going to be a long night."

Abe watched as Russell stood up and stretched before grabbing the nearly empty glass and walking toward the kitchen. It was obvious by the other man's gait that he didn't want to leave Celina's side.

While he was gone, Abe quickly checked to be sure Celina hadn't started bleeding again. He had just covered her back up when Russell returned with a fresh glass of water. He relaxed when he had returned to the kitchen. At least she wasn't bleeding. That was a good sign if nothing else.

Several minutes later, Russell returned to check on them. "Any change?"

"No. I did check her a few minutes ago, and she's not bleeding."

"Good. That's something, right?" Russell ran a hand through his hair. "Soup will be ready in about an hour. Do you want some coffee?"

"Yeah. That would be good." Abe sighed as he continued to read.

He heard Russell's boots scrape on the wood floor as he turned around and walked back to the other room. He wished he had something else positive to tell the other man, but the truth was, Celina was in serious shape. He watched the shallow rise and fall of her chest with each breath she took. He checked either side of her neck to see if her veins were pulsing as if her blood pressure might be up like the book talked about. They didn't look any different than usual as far as he could tell.

While he waited for Russell to return with coffee, Abe coaxed small amounts of water down Celina's throat, praying he didn't choke her in the process. He checked her ankles and felt like they had gone down some since they had placed a pillow under her feet to lift them off the mattress some. He found himself rubbing lightly over her rounded belly beneath the covers as he continued reading in the book. For some reason, it soothed him to touch her there. It was while he was smoothing over her belly that he felt the kick that told him the baby was alive. He hadn't been very hopeful after cleaning up all the blood.

"Hey! You're smiling. What is it? Did she wake up?" Russell hurried around the couch and handed Abe one of the mugs he was carrying.

"No, but I felt the baby kick."

Russell grinned and quickly slipped his hand beneath the covers to cover the opposite side of Celina's belly. After a few seconds, both men felt the baby's kick again. They grinned at each other like fools.

"It's a good sign, right?" Russell asked.

"I think it is. As long as it's moving around, we know it's alive."

"Is something wrong with my baby?" Celina's weak voice startled both of them.

Abe instantly turned to cup her cheek with his trembling hand. Relief poured over him in warm waves that threatened to loosen the tears that had been gathering all afternoon.

Chapter Thirteen

"No, no. You're the one we've been worried about. You wouldn't wake up for us."

"I don't understand." She moved to sit up, but Russell immediately stopped her.

"Easy, sweetness. Just be still and rest. We think your blood pressure has been getting too high and that's why your feet and ankles are swelling."

"Have you had a headache, baby?" Abe asked.

"Off and on for a few days now. Nothing real bad. Mostly my back has been hurting."

"You're going to have to start resting more. You've been on your feet too much." Abe's expression might have been frightening when she had first met him, but not anymore.

"I was resting earlier. I remember lying down on the couch and Russell wanted me to drink some water." She looked around. Not only was she no longer on the couch, but she didn't have anything on other than her overly large shirt.

"What happened to my clothes?"

She watched as the two men exchanged panicked glances. Something more had happened than what they were telling her. She narrowed her eyes at Russell. He was the easiest to manipulate when she wanted something.

"Russell. What are you trying to keep from me? You know how I feel about lying."

"Nothing, Celina. You don't need to worry or get upset. It will just drive your blood pressure up again and that could be dangerous."

Abe moved so that her view of the other man was blocked. "Are you hungry?"

"What I am is pissed. I want to know what you're not telling me." She tried to push him out of the way.

"Abe. She needs to know." Russell pulled the other man back and stared at him. "We can't hide things from her."

"You better listen to Russell. I've told both of you that I can't abide lying, whether by omission or words. Don't do it, Abe." Celina reached out and clasped his wrist in hopes he would look into her eyes.

She watched as he struggled with what he thought was best for her and what she wanted. He finally turned and looked at her. With an audible sigh all of the tension that had been evident in the tightness around his mouth and through his shoulders dissipated. He should have felt relief, but Celina was pretty sure he only felt defeated in what he thought of as his duty to her.

"We had to clean you up, Celina. When Russell found you, you'd been bleeding vaginally. We were scared you had lost the baby, but the bleeding had already stopped and it looked much worse than it was."

She gasped, her hands immediately going to cover her belly. She held her hands there, praying that the baby would move or kick to calm her racing heart. Even as she fought to relax, her breathing began to quicken.

"See, you're getting upset. It's the worst thing in the world for you to do, baby." Abe soothed his hand over her forehead.

"I don't feel the baby moving. Something's wrong!" Her voice rose in a quiver.

"Shh, Celina," Russell said. "We were feeling the little thing kicking when you woke up. He's probably tired now."

She nodded and tried to calm down once again. They were right. Getting upset would only make things worse. She struggled to stop the tears that leaked from her eyes despite her attempts to stop them.

"He's probably a she, you know." Celina knew it would distract both men from her poor attempt to stop crying.

"No way. The good Lord wouldn't torment us that way. Can you imagine another little Celina running around, keeping us hopping?" Russell asked, poking Abe on the shoulder.

"Hell, we can't handle one. There's no way we could deal with two." Abe stared toward the fire as he spoke.

With one last sniffle, Celina managed to dry her eyes and settle down once again. Her eyelids drooped low even as she tried to remain awake. She was scared to fall asleep again. What if she started bleeding again and didn't realize it?

"Abe?"

He looked down and met her gaze once again. "What is it, Celina?"

"I'm scared. Don't let anything happen to my baby."

* * * *

Abe's heart shot into his throat at her simple request. Nothing had ever been more out of his reach than promising her he wouldn't let anything happen to either of them. Still, he uttered soft placating words so she would relax and go to sleep. He had no business making promises he had no control over. He ground his teeth and stood up.

"Stay with her, Russell. Don't leave her side. I'm going to take care of the animals. We'll have to take turns watching her from now on. I don't want her to be alone anymore. It's too dangerous."

"What about the soup? You haven't eaten yet."

"I'll eat when I get back. Go fix a bowl for yourself while I get ready to go out. We can warm it back up when I get back. Celina will need to eat as well."

Russell nodded and walked to the kitchen as Abe stared down at Celina. She still looked far too pale for his peace of mind. Despite having gained weight over the last few months, she still appeared frail and tiny compared to him.

Turning, he shuffled over to where their outer clothes hung on pegs by the door. He slipped into everything except his gloves and scarf, waiting for Russell to return before he added those last two articles of clothing. Despite how cold it was outside, it was still too warm inside to stand around fully clothed for the outside.

Russell hurried out of the kitchen carrying a bowl and a glass. He settled on the floor next to the mattress and balanced the soup on his knee. Abe nodded at him and pulled on his gloves before opening the door. The brisk wind nearly jerked the heavy door from his grasp. He closed it with a solid thump and wrapped his scarf around his neck as he trudged toward the barn. At least it wasn't snowing again. He would take any gift he could get at this point.

The entire time he worked in the barn tending to the horses, his thoughts kept drifting back to Celina and how much she meant to them. In such a short time, he'd somehow let her into his heart and the thought of losing her nearly brought him to his knees. What had happened to never allowing anyone to get close enough to have that effect on him again? Where had he dropped the ball and allowed it to happen?

I never had a chance. She's too pretty and wouldn't give up on me.

Abe scoffed at his early intentions of keeping her at arm's length. If the truth were told, he hadn't tried nearly hard enough.

Face it. I wanted a chance at happiness again, but I wanted the choice to be taken away from me. I'm nothing but a coward.

When he had finished in the barn, Abe checked on the herd. The water trough had frozen over again. He broke the ice then walked as much of the fence line as possible to assure there were no breaks that would allow the cows to wander off during the night. All they needed was to lose their major source of meat. At least their milk cow was doing well. If Celina wasn't able to breastfeed, they would need the cow's milk.

A vision of her nestling a babe to her breast nearly dropped him to his knees. She would be beautiful caring for the child. Feelings of protectiveness and maybe even a little possessiveness filled him. When he thought about it, he realized that he considered Russell as an extension of himself and those feelings didn't apply to him. He expected Russell to help him keep her safe.

He continued tending to chores but couldn't stop thinking about Celina and how good she felt between him and Russell each night. She lamented her rounded body like most pregnant women, but it didn't stop him from wanting her. His cock hardened, and thoughts of how much her breasts had grown over the last few months tightened his balls. Hell. If he didn't get his thoughts on something less erotic, he was going to come in his pants.

It had been a few days since they had played any with Celina. She had become increasingly more uncomfortable. Neither man wanted to risk hurting her or the baby. Instead, they took care of themselves in the shower each night before bed.

As he finished up by checking the chickens to be sure they had plenty of food and that there weren't any holes that a fox or wolf could push through, Abe headed for the wood pile. He needed to get inside and relieve Russell for a while.

The entire time he'd been outside, he hadn't allowed his mind to focus on the one thing he needed to think about. What did he really feel for Celina? He cared about her and wanted her to be happy. He'd flirted with the idea that he was a little bit in love with her, but deep down he knew it was more than a little bit. His heart had been involved almost from the beginning, but he could no longer deny the connection his soul felt with her now. She'd captured the one piece of him he thought he would never relinquish again. Hell, for years he hadn't even thought he had a soul anymore. She had arrived and proved to him that he did, and now she owned it.

Did he dare tell her what she meant to him? As long as he kept that one small secret safe, she wouldn't have the power to destroy him. Once he shared her importance in his life with her, she could crush him with a careless word or a thoughtless look.

Dropping the last log on the pile outside the door, Abe brushed off the dirt and snow from his coat and opened the door to the lodge. Almost as soon as he had closed the door, a feeling of peace settled in around him. He could see Russell holding Celina's hand with their heads close together talking about something. The warmth from the fire reached across the room to help battle the cooler air that had hitched a ride inside with him.

Once he had removed all of his outerwear and left his boots at the door, he padded over to the fire and turned his back to it with his hands behind him. Celina looked up from the book she and Russell were reading together. He had propped her up against the couch with a pillow and was holding the book for her.

"Everything okay with the animals?" Russell asked.

"Fine. The herd is keeping close to the fence, and the chickens were quiet for a change."

"I'll go warm the soup back up. Celina was just saying she was hungry." Russell stood up and stretched.

They all laughed when his knees creaked with the effort. He ruffled Celina's hair before strolling across the room and through the kitchen door. Abe watched the parade of emotions that crossed Celina's expressive face. He couldn't begin to decipher all of them. What was she thinking? Did it have anything to do with him?

"The baby moved for me a little while ago. She's okay in there." He watched as she smoothed a hand over her belly on top of the covers.

"Told you *he* was." He watched her brow arch at his emphasis on the "he."

"You know I haven't really thought about baby names. I need to do that. I don't think I really have much longer according to the books Russell and I've been reading through."

"I can't believe we haven't been researching this all along." Abe shook his head.

It had been stupid and dangerous to hide his head in the sand all this time. If they didn't focus on her pregnancy, they could almost forget she was going to have a baby one day in the future. Well, that future date was fast approaching and they were floundering around in the dark now. Shame heated his face as, once again, he called himself a coward.

"I'm the one who should have been trying to figure out what was going on with me. I mean, it's my body. I think I've been too scared to let myself think about it. For a while I felt like I was all alone, and focusing on being pregnant was too scary for me. Then, we all started getting closer, and I didn't want to lose that by harping on having a baby. I was being selfish and wanted to hold on to how good I felt being with you and Russell."

He moved closer to her and dropped to his knees on the mattress next to her. He couldn't stand to see the sadness in her eyes. She should be happy right now.

"We're to blame, baby. Not you. We should have made it clear that our relationship included the baby. We failed to give you what you needed. It was our job to make sure you were happy and content. That meant making sure you felt safe not only as a woman, but as a mother to be, too. I'm sorry, Celina." Abe kissed her forehead and rested his chin on top of her head.

Russell appeared with two bowls of soup in his hands. Abe stood up and took one of the bowls, setting it on the table by the couch before grabbing the other one and giving it to Celina.

"I'll be right back with something to drink for both of you." Russell hurried back into the kitchen.

Abe settled next to Celina and waited for her to start eating. When she didn't immediately take a spoonful, he cocked his head to the side and nodded at the bowl.

She smiled and lifted a spoonful of the soup to her mouth and blew on it before taking a sip of the liquid. She hummed her appreciation as Russell returned with two glasses of milk. Abe frowned at the other man, but Russell just smiled and nodded toward Celina. Fine, he could handle drinking milk with the soup as long as he got a cup of coffee before he went to bed.

While they ate, Russell talked about the baby and what all they needed to be doing to get ready. It was then that Abe realized what Celina had been saying earlier. They hadn't done a single thing to prepare for the new life that would soon be a part of their group, their family. He could remember all of the preparations he and his wife had made for their children. By the last child, they had most everything down to a fine art. This was Celina's first child, and they had pretty much robbed her of all of the hoopla that normally surrounded the birth of a child.

He looked at her as she finished her milk. Guilt washed over him once again. She deserved so much more than he had offered her.

If only...

Well, he couldn't turn back time. All he could do was make sure the remainder of her pregnancy went smoothly and that she had everything she needed for the baby.

"I'm thinking of Samantha if it's a girl and Sam if it's a boy. What do you guys think?"

Abe tried not to cringe. At her sudden frown, he knew he hadn't succeeded. Russell came to the rescue.

"I like Lindsey Ann for a girl and Aiden Matthew for a boy."

"What do you think, Abe?" Celina asked turning to him.

"Candice would be a pretty name, and I'm with Russell on Aiden Matthew. That's a strong name. A boy needs a strong name."

Celina laughed. The happy sound did things to his cock and lifted the cloud that had settled around him earlier. Somehow it filled the great room with a warmth that had nothing to do with the massive fire roaring in the hearth.

"I think we need to clean out the master bedroom and move in there once spring gets here and that little room next to it should be the nursery." Russell had settled down on the other side of Celina after setting her empty bowl on the table next to the couch.

Abe's mouth went dry. He hadn't thought about what they would do once there was no longer a need to remain downstairs any longer. Between the wintery cold and Celina's advanced pregnancy, he'd been content to remain sleeping together in front of the fire. Though he'd toyed with the thought that come spring they would continue their sleeping arrangement, he hadn't really committed himself to the idea.

Idiot. What did I think would happen, that we would all just go happily back to sleeping in our own rooms—alone?

"What do you think, Abe?" Celina's soft voice warned him that he'd missed something important.

"Ah, sorry. I was thinking about all the stuff in that room that we are going to have to move. What were you saying?"

The relief on Russell's face told him that the other man had expected him to screw that up. Now he was almost afraid to find out what he'd missed hearing, because this time he would have to answer her.

"I was just saying that maybe we should start working on that right away. Once the baby gets here, I won't be able to help much at first and you're going to be busy with chores and getting the garden ready to plant." Her eyes shined bright with excitement.

Abe could have basked in her happiness forever. He had no desire to see it dim. He had no choice but to agree with her. It wasn't that he didn't want to continue sleeping with her. It was that it was all moving toward becoming a real family faster than the speed of light to him. If he were honest, though, it really hadn't moved very fast to begin with, though it certainly was making up for lost time now.

Nodding, he smiled at her. "I think you're right. We need to get started before things get crazy busy. Russell and I will work on it tomorrow."

"I'm going to help." Celina's lower lip stuck out just the smallest amount.

"Baby. You have to rest and keep off of your feet. Besides, you have no business going up and down those stairs. It's too dangerous. You might fall." Abe frowned at her.

The tighter his mouth became, the farther her lips poked out until he thought he would melt away with guilt. What was it about a woman's pouty mouth and teary eyes that got a man to agree to things he never would have normally? Had to be the thought of those lips wrapped around his dick that made him lose his head for the few seconds it took the woman to get what she wanted out of him.

"If you're doing okay in the morning after we finish chores, we will help you up the stairs, but you have to sit or lay on the bed while we do the work." Abe scowled at Russell as if the other man was the root cause of all of his problems with Celina.

Russell smirked before quickly covering his mouth with his hand when Abe glowered in his direction again.

"I can live with that. Then we have to figure out how to set the nursery up." Celina seemed oblivious to Abe's distress.

Chapter Fourteen

Over the next two weeks, the men worked tirelessly to get the master bedroom cleaned out, moving all of their combined things into the one room. Then they started work on the nursery next to it. All during this time, Celina directed from the comforts of the bed or a chair, chafing at the bit to handle things herself. She was tired of doing nothing and seeing the men working so hard. Between taking care of everything outside, seeing to her needs, and rearranging furniture, she didn't see how they managed to get up each morning to start over again.

The weather proved to grow steadily warmer until suddenly the snow seemed like a distant memory. Though the nights continued to be quite cold, the days were blessedly warmer and Celina badgered the men every chance she had to let her go outside for a few minutes. Even as she begged, she felt guilty harassing them like she did. All of the conflicting emotions kept her in constant turmoil, sending the men into fits about her health.

"Please, Abe. I need fresh air at least once a day."

"Celina, I don't like taking you outside like that in your condition. All the excitement and moving around isn't good for you."

He ran a hand over his face when she pouted prettily up at him. "Fine. Russell and I will go with you once he gets back in from doing chores. Just for a few minutes, Celina."

"Thank you!"

"I swear you're more trouble than you're worth." He scowled down at her, but she could see the teasing in his eyes.

She had no doubts that the men cared about her and quite possibly even loved her on some level. She wouldn't push them on it, though. They would tell her when the time was right for them. She could respect their loyalty to their previous families. She'd had Roger and knew the difficulty of relegating her past life and love to another spot in her heart to make room for her men.

Her men. She smiled at that thought. They were her men, and she was their woman. She could live with that.

"Time to head downstairs and make sure the shepherd's pie is ready for lunch." Abe picked her up as if she weighed nothing and carefully carried her out of the nursery and down the stairs where he sat her on the couch in front of the hearth.

They kept a smaller fire going despite the fact that the days were warmer. Abe seemed obsessed with making sure she didn't catch a cold. While he disappeared into the kitchen to get ready for lunch, Celina pulled off the extra shirt he insisted she wear when they were upstairs away from the fireplace. Today her back was aching again, and though she didn't think it was anything serious, she felt as if she should tell the men. Maybe after lunch—after they went outside. She smiled. She wanted her time out in the fresh air and sunshine first.

The door opened, and Russell walked in. She smiled as she turned to watch him hang up his jacket and slip out of his boots. The ready grin on his face when he saw her heated her skin.

"There's my favorite woman. Did you get a lot done in the nursery this morning?" He leaned over and kissed her before rubbing lightly on her tummy.

"Well, Abe did. I just watched and made sure he did it right."

"I wish we could manage to find a baby bed." His brows drew together as he frowned.

"Don't worry so much about it. The deep drawer from the chest is perfect. We can carry her from room to room until she outgrows it."

"Where's Abe?" Russell asked, looking around.

"In the kitchen. We're having shepherd's pie for lunch." Celina laughed when her stomach growled.

"Sounds like someone's hungry." Russell chuckled and scooped her up in his arms.

"I can walk, Russell! It's just to the kitchen." She slapped his shoulder playfully.

"No need to walk when you can ride."

When he pushed open the kitchen door and walked through, Abe looked up from where he'd been sitting at the table, a steaming cup of coffee in his hands. Guilt slid across his face like a sea serpent. Russell's eyebrow arched, but he didn't say anything. Celina knew they both snuck around and drank their coffee behind her back. It really didn't bother her anymore. She knew coffee was bad for the baby, but it was almost a necessity for the men. They needed it to keep warm and to stay alert when they were working outside. She felt a bit guilty herself for having made such a big deal out of it before.

Once Russell had settled her in a chair at the table, she eased out of her seat and climbed onto Abe's lap. She leaned back and smiled up at him. It didn't take long for her to coax a small smile from him. Then she stretched up and kissed him softly on the lips. After a second of hesitation, Abe wrapped his arms tightly around her and pulled her as close to him as her generous belly would allow. He nuzzled her neck, inhaling deeply as he did. She loved that he seemed to enjoy breathing her in.

"I'm starved. Is lunch ready? Can I take it out of the oven?" Russell asked, interrupting their cuddle session.

"It's ready. I've already turned off the oven. Just pull it out and set it on the table. We can dip out of it." Abe didn't move from where he had his nose buried against her neck.

"I think I understood that." Russell chuckled. "I'm slowly learning to speak mumble around you."

Celina giggled. "I've gotten to where I can pick up the meaning of some of his grunts."

"You both suck." Abe pulled back, and after dropping a quick kiss to her lips, he moved her over to her chair.

Celina eyed the heaping spoonful of the meaty pie Russell had added to her plate. Just a few minutes ago, she'd felt as if she could eat a cow all by herself. Now she didn't feel as hungry. In fact, she felt a little sick at her stomach.

While the men cleaned their plates, she moved her food around to make it look like she was eating more than she was. Hopefully they wouldn't notice and start worrying over her like mother hens. She'd never have believed that those two men would worry over her as much as they did if she hadn't been the recipient of their over protectiveness.

Thankfully, they were arguing over getting the garden ready to plant as they cleaned up the dishes and didn't pay attention to her lack of appetite. By the time they had finished straightening the kitchen, she felt much better and was looking forward to her trip outside.

"I'm ready to go out whenever you are." She smiled up at the two men when they put away the dishcloths.

"Patience, baby." Abe tweaked her nose. "We'll get there."

Russell smiled before picking her up and carrying her back to the great room. Instead of heading directly for the couch, he walked over to the door and stood her up so she could pull on her coat. She could tell her face was beaming by the indulgent smile on his face. Abe helped her slip into her boots. Then the three of them walked outside into the sunshine and fresh air.

Celina leaned her head back and gloried in the feel of the sun on her face. It smelled wonderful out there. She knew she wasn't a prisoner, but sometimes it sure felt like it. These brief periods of time when she cold bask in the freedom of nature helped her handle the harshness of her situation. It wouldn't be much longer and she wouldn't be this fragile anymore. It was just because she was pregnant and had gotten sick.

"Come on, sweetness. Let's get you settled. You don't need to be standing on your feet." Russell helped her waddle over to the chair they had built just for her.

The rough-hewed wood had been fashioned to support her back, and when they added the pillow they always brought out with them, it was almost as comfortable as the couch. Their thoughtfulness always amazed her.

While they were outside, Abe and Russell walked over the garden area and talked more about enlarging it. She was sure they were thinking about the fact that now there were three of them, soon to be four. Of course her baby wouldn't exactly be eating anything out of it for a while.

The soft breeze, though a bit chilly, felt wonderful as it lifted her hair and teased at her cheeks. She couldn't wait for warmer weather where she could spend more time outside and introduce her baby to everything. She had little doubt that her men would be just as resistant to letting her carry her baby outside as they were to her going out now. She smiled to herself. She would find ways around them. She knew how to distract them when she needed to.

Her back began to ache again, only this time the pain seemed to inch around her sides some now. Soon it became too uncomfortable to just sit still. She stood up and stretched hoping the movement would ease the discomfort.

"Are you okay, Celina?" Abe hurried over to her.

"I'm fine, just stiff."

"Don't lie to us. You look like you're in pain." Russell's serious expression said that he wasn't buying her explanation one bit.

"My back is a little sore today is all. I can't seem to be still in one place for long."

"Time to go inside and lie down." Abe's tone brooked no argument.

He deftly picked her up and carried her back inside. He didn't even stop by the back door to pull off her coat or boots. He carried her straight up the stairs and to the master bedroom. They hadn't slept in the big room yet. They had been still sleeping in front of the fireplace on the mattress.

"I think it's time we moved upstairs to sleep now. It's warm enough at night with all three of us in the bed." Abe smiled down at her as he settled her in the bed after Russell pulled down the covers.

They each pulled off a boot, and then Russell removed her coat and helped her out of her pants. She squirmed, trying to find a comfortable position, but her back truly ached now. She'd read that toward the end of the pregnancy she would find it nearly impossible to get comfortable. She hadn't truly appreciated that until now.

"How about a back rub, sweetness?" Russell toed off his boots and climbed on the bed behind her.

The first touch of his hands to her lower back was like a healing balm. She moaned with appreciation as he nimbly manipulated her muscles. He seemed to know exactly how to ease the tenseness that had settled there.

"Does that feel better, baby?" Abe asked.

Lines etched his features, telling her he was worried about her. She didn't want him upset. She was fine.

"Much better. I may take a little nap." She yawned and closed her eyes.

"I'll be downstairs if you need me." Abe's footsteps grew fainter as he left the room.

Celina relaxed deeper into the mattress while Russell worked magic on her back. The soothing motions of his fingers soon lulled her into a welcome sleep. Her only thought was that she prayed she wouldn't have to suffer with her back for much longer.

* * * *

He watched her face slowly relax as he peered over her shoulder while he carefully manipulated the muscles of her back. Russell hated seeing her in any sort of pain. He couldn't imagine how he would handle it when she actually went into labor. Just the thought of it sent chills down his spine. The fact that she was having back pains already worried him. It could be a sign of early labor. He'd been reading up on childbirth in the books lately. He didn't want to be unprepared when the time came.

Right now she seemed to be resting fairly comfortably. Still, she was close to term, and every little distress built the knowledge inside of him that the worst was yet to come. There would be nothing he could do to help ease the pain.

He gently brushed the hair from her face and soaked up her peaceful expression. He could look at her for hours on end. Her strength and determination to help do her share around the place had drawn him to her originally. The beauty and strength in her heart had anchored him and locked him to her for all time. Russell knew he loved her. He had never really denied it to himself in the first place. Maybe he had tiptoed around it in the beginning, but mostly because she had just lost her husband and pushing her would have been insensitive, not to mention rude.

Still, he hadn't been able to keep his heart from becoming engaged from almost the beginning. She made him smile, and he hadn't had much reason to smile when they had first met. Something about her had crept under his skin and set up house until he finally acknowledged that she meant something to him.

From there, it didn't take long until he'd found himself in love and happy about it. Seeing Abe slowly accept her and then become entranced by her only tightened the hold she had around his heart.

He wondered what was different this time when before, he hadn't wanted to share his wife and that was ultimately what had gotten her killed. Why was he okay with sharing Celina with Abe when he hadn't wanted to let another man touch his first wife? Did he love Celina less? Russell couldn't believe that. It had to be that he loved her differently. Or maybe it was as simple as he had grown and reconciled with himself the necessity of it for her safety.

Whatever the reason, Russell was eternally grateful for the other man's willingness to share in both her loving nature and the responsibility of keeping her safe. Her happiness mattered more to him than just about anything. Seeing her smile brought a joy to his heart he cherished. He vowed that no matter what it took, he would strive to keep that smile there for the rest of her life.

Her soft snore tugged at his lips. He couldn't help but smile at the normality. He slowly eased down on the bed next to her and curled around her. He would take a quick nap with her. The next thing he knew, he was sound asleep.

Chapter Fifteen

Pain stabbing around her belly dragged Celina out of the perfectly sinful dream she'd been having involving both Russell and Abe and a pair of fur-lined handcuffs. She gasped for breath as the pain prevented her from drawing in a complete one. Then it eased and she panted against the pillow she had buried her face in.

"Celina? What's wrong?" Russell's worried voice startled her. She hadn't realized he was still in bed with her.

She started to speak when another pain gripped her in a steel trap of misery. She moaned instead. Russell almost immediately began to massage her back. It helped, but it wasn't giving her nearly as much relief as it had earlier. Nausea threatened to overwhelm her as once again the pain began to ebb.

"I don't know. I think I might be in labor. The pain was mostly in my back, but now it's more in my belly."

"Don't move. I'm going to get Abe. Just stay right there." He jumped out of bed and hurried out the door in his sock feet.

He wasn't gone long before she heard him calling down the stairs for Abe to bring the pregnancy book and come upstairs. Then he was right back by her side, gently rubbing small circles around her swollen belly. She had to admit it felt wonderful. At least for the time being.

"What's going on?" Abe asked as he rushed into the room.

She noted that he had both of the pregnancy books that they'd begun to rely on in his arms. Before she could reassure him, another pain seized her, and she moaned.

"She's having back and stomach pains." Russell's voice held a quiver to it.

"Fuck! We need to time them." Abe's didn't sound any stronger.

"How the hell can we time them without a damn watch?"

"Count between them. It's the best we can do."

Celina wanted to scream at them to be quiet. She didn't need their panic right now. She needed some strength, and maybe some morphine. She tried to breathe around the pain, but it was hard. She'd never felt anything like the squeezing agony that clamped down on her belly.

"How long have you been hurting like this?" Abe asked, desperately flipping pages in one of the books.

"I think it just started," Russell answered for her.

"My back has been hurting off and on all day."

Both men froze and stared at her. She wanted to scream at them to stop screwing around and do something, but she knew there was nothing they could do. This was all on her.

"Why didn't you say something?" Abe demanded.

"I didn't think it was that bad and what can you do about it anyway?" Celina was fast losing patience with them.

"Well, we could have given you more back rubs," Russell sputtered.

She scoffed at that suggestion. While she could use one right now, she wasn't about to ask for it. At least not yet. She wasn't so sure her bravado would last much longer, though. The pain was getting more intense with each bout of contractions. She had resigned herself to the fact that she was in labor. While a part of her deep down was excited to finally be able to meet her baby, another part of her was frightened out of her skull.

This time when the contraction squeezed down on her belly and lower back, Celina cried out. Both of the men stilled with answering looks of pain on their faces. She almost wished she could draw in enough breath to reassure them. Truth be known, though, she really just wanted to be able to breathe comfortably and rest.

"How far apart are they?" Abe asked Russell.

"I don't know. I forgot to count."

"Damn it, Russell. You've got to keep up with them."

"Don't yell at him, Abe." She finally drew in a deep breath and closed her eyes.

"Rest, baby. We're going to take care of you." Abe kissed her sweaty brow.

Celina wanted to laugh at them, but they were trying, and all she really wanted was for them to hold her and for the pain to go away. As if in answer to her prayers, Russell got up on the bed and scooted around her back. With the first touch of his hands at her back, a moan escaped her lips.

Abe hurried around them setting up the room for the delivery. At some point he roused her to drape a tarp underneath her to protect the bed. She was almost hyperaware of everything around her. She was sure it had something to do with the endorphins cruising around in her bloodstream. Whatever the reason, she was ecstatic. This felt more like the high she'd experienced after getting a good dose of laughing gas at the dentist's office.

"Breathe, sweetness, breathe." Russell immediately began to soothe over her back with his warm hands. He'd felt her stiffen and immediately reacted to it.

Celina didn't have any idea how long they had been upstairs, but she was so tired and wanted to take a nap. When she closed her eyes, Adam's shout had her jerking her eyes open to stare into his slightly wild ones.

"Your water broke! This is it, baby. You've got to concentrate now."

She couldn't help but roll her eyes before she let them drift closed once again. Less than a minute later, though, another pain hit, and she nearly screamed with this one. All the panting in the world wasn't going to help her live through this. Celina clenched her teeth as fear that she'd die gripped her throat almost as fiercely as the labor pains squeezed her abdomen. Her legs cramped with trying to press into the mattress to escape some of the pressure.

"They're about three minutes apart, Abe." Russell's excited voice broke through the haze of pain and desperation.

Celina wanted to scream at them that this wasn't working. She wanted to stop and do something different, but she knew there wasn't any stopping the labor. She rested between bouts of earth-shattering cramps that made her think all of her insides were going to be born with the baby. Russell brushed her wet hair away from her face and kissed her cheek as he massaged her shoulders. She wanted to tell him that it wasn't helping anything, but that would have been mean. He was just trying to support her, and his back rubs did help some during the labor pains.

She could hear them talking over her as she drifted between rounds. God, please let her baby be okay. That was all that mattered in the long run. She ached to hold her child in her arms and prayed that it would all be over soon. She was so tired.

Then another wave of the intense pressure and pain hit her. She screamed as she fought it.

* * * *

"Here you go, mommy. All cleaned up and hungry." Abe gently laid the tiny squirming bundle in Celina's arms.

"She's beautiful. Isn't she?" Celina looked up into his eyes.

"She's perfect. You did good, baby. What did you decide to name her?" Abe asked.

"Bethany Ann. I'll call her Beth for short."

Abe looked over at Russell. They both laughed. She hadn't used any of the names they'd talked about after all. He liked that she'd chosen a name after holding her in her arms. Beth would be a beautiful woman one day, and he prayed for the strength to keep her and her momma safe. Seeing her born had been one of the most wonderful experiences of his life. Though he'd always made it home for his children's births, he'd never been in the delivery room to see the event. Now he mourned that loss.

Glancing away from the sight of baby Beth suckling at Celina's breast, he met Russell's gaze and they both smiled like idiots. They might not have fathered this child, but she would be loved and cared for as if they had. Maybe, if they were lucky, there would be another one someday that carried their blood in his veins.

"Her fingers are so tiny. Look at the itty bity fingernails." The awe in Celina's voice was just as precious at the little bundle she held safe in her arms.

"All I can see is how ferociously she is sucking on that nipple." Abe chuckled at her quick eye roll.

"Leave it to you to focus on that. I swear, you and Russell have boobs on the brain."

"I'll admit to it," Russell said with a straight face. "I enjoy watching those luscious breasts move when one of us is fucking you."

"Don't remind me," Abe said with a groan. "Six more weeks of blue balls is probably going to leave me permanently disfigured."

Celina's warm laughter filled his heart. She was beautiful with her mussed hair flying in all different directions and those tear-stained cheeks. Just the sight of her relaxing there with Beth nestled against her was enough to bring tears to his eyes. He turned away and started cleaning up.

"Abe. I'll do that. You sit here with Celina and rub her belly some. The book said we need to be sure her womb shrinks back down to slow the bleeding. The baby feeding at her breast will help, but we don't have any of the medication they give to help her."

Abe blinked back the tears and turned around as Russell extracted himself carefully from behind Celina's back.

"You don't have to clean it all up alone. I'll help with it."

"I think I need to change breasts. Abe, can you help me? I'm scared I'll drop her." Celina's anxious voice galvanized him into action.

He quickly slipped in bed with her and helped her adjust baby Bethany to her other breast. The baby squirmed a bit at being interrupted but soon settled back down to nurse. He could only stare over Celina's shoulder as the little thing latched onto her nipple and sucked like a champ.

"What does it feel like?" Abe asked in a hushed voice.

"Strange. It hurt a little at first, but now it's not so bad. It's a drawing sensation. I can't explain it but I feel so close to her like this. Knowing that I'm providing her with what she needs is a big rush. I want to always be able to give her what she needs."

"We all do, baby. Russell and I will always provide for you both. If you'll let us, we'll be her fathers as if she was of our blood." Abe stopped.

He hadn't meant to spring that on her so soon, and definitely not without Russell there with him. The other man had taken the dirty towels and sheets out of the room and hadn't returned yet. He sighed and ran his hand up and down Celina's upper arms. She relaxed against him, and he could almost feel the baby sucking at her breast through her body as it rested against his.

The other man slipped back into the room and continued gathering the supplies and returning the unused portion to the bathroom and other areas of the house. He'd piled everything into the room just in case he needed it. Now the room would look bare without them there. The soft smile on Russell's face warmed Abe. He liked knowing his family was safe and happy surrounding him. For now, that was all that mattered. They would have to discuss the process of keeping them both safe in the future.

Abe wasn't sure how long they sat like that while the baby fed, but once Celina had placed the tiny bundle over her shoulder to burp her, he figured it was time for both mommy and infant to get some much-needed rest. Maybe they all need to rest after all that had occurred. He had noticed the shadows beneath Russell's eyes. He was sure his face wasn't all that much better.

"I think a nap is in order, guys. What do y'all think?" He noticed Russell's instant smile as he smoothed out the sheets that he could reach on the bed.

"Sounds good to me. Celina looks as if she's about to fall over now." He reached for the baby, and for an instant, he wasn't sure she would let Russell have her.

"Feeling a little protective?" Abe asked playfully.

"I didn't think it would be so hard just to put her down to sleep. Silly, isn't it?" She finally released her hold on baby Beth.

Russell immediately removed the child from her arms and settled her in the makeshift crib they'd made out of a deep drawer. It would keep the baby safe. She couldn't roll out of it, and they could place it right next to the bed for easy reach. As soon as he had settled her in and covered her up, he stood up and undressed down to his boxers and climbed under the covers to snuggle up against their woman.

Abe smiled. Their woman, and she was. He removed his clothes and got in on the other side of Celina. He felt her sigh as he nuzzled her neck with his mouth.

"I love you, Abe." She looked over to where Russell lay with his head watching her. "I love you, Russell. I never thought I could love again, but you two showed me that though Roger will still be in my heart, there is plenty of room for you both there as well. I wouldn't give any part of our relationship away."

Abe felt his chest constrict. She loved them. She'd actually said the words out loud, and even he could hear the sincerity in her voice. He needed to tell her how he felt, but it seemed too trite to follow up her declaration with his own. He looked over at Russell. His friend seemed to be mulling over his options as well. Their eyes met, and almost as if they could speak in each other's minds, they both knew that now wasn't the right time to confess their love for her and her child.

* * * *

She could feel the love radiating from them as they surrounded her and Beth. She knew without them telling her that they loved her. She held no doubt in her heart that they loved Bethany just as much. It was all in their eyes as they gazed down at the little being wrapped in the tiny blanket Russell had created just for her. Knowing that they would watch over them, Celina tried to rest, but her heart was too full and her mind busy thinking about everything she wanted to do.

She must have dozed at some point, because suddenly she was wide awake and Bethany wasn't in her arms. She panicked that she had dropped her and tried to get up to look for her.

"Whoa there. You need to go slow so that you don't hurt yourself. You just gave birth a few hours ago, sweetness." Russell wrapped his arms around her.

"Where's Bethany?" She tried to move out of his arms to find her baby.

"Shhh, you'll wake her up. She's sleeping in her bed right there." Russell pointed to the end of the bed where the makeshift crib had been settled against the footboard to keep it secure. "Abe settled her there after changing her diaper."

She let out a sigh of relief. "He changed her diaper?"

Somehow the sight of the big mountain of a man fooling with something so tiny seemed absurd and she smothered a laugh.

"He's pretty good at it. Don't forget that we've both had children before." Russell kissed her cheek.

"His hands are so large. I just couldn't picture him using a safety pin without sticking himself."

"Well, I didn't say he got by uninjured." Russell's deep chuckle sent her into another fit of giggles.

She realized that her entire body was sore. She moaned and clutched her belly.

"What's wrong? Are you hurting?" Russell immediately grew serious.

"I'm okay. I'm just sore all over. I'll get over it. I better get a shower before Beth wakes up and is hungry."

Russell helped her ease out of the bed. "I'm surprised she's slept this long."

"Check her for me. Just to be sure she's breathing." Fear slithered like a snake down her spine. How could she have slept without checking on her baby?

"She's fine. Sleeping like a lamb. I can see her breathing." He walked back over to her and helped her shuffle into the bathroom.

After turning on the shower to let it get warm, Russell helped her undress and then peeled out of his clothes as well. She wasn't surprised that he wouldn't let her shower without him there to watch her. It was actually a relief to know that he wouldn't let her fall if she lost her balance or slipped. Her legs felt like noodles, and she wasn't sure how long she would be able to stand up on her own.

"Let's get you cleaned up and back in bed." He helped her inside the enclosure and followed her in.

He quickly washed her then held her as she stood under the soothing hot water to rinse off. Once out of the shower, he blotted her skin dry with a soft towel. Just as they walked back into the bedroom, Beth let out an angry scream. They both stopped in their tracks at the loud noise that erupted from the tiny bundle in the drawer.

"I'll get her." Russell helped Celina climb into bed before hurrying around to lift the thrashing infant out of her bed. "Easy there, sweet Bethany. Momma has your dinner nice and warm for you."

"Russell!" Celina couldn't help the smile that formed at his irreverent words.

He handed her his precious bundle with a grin, but didn't say anything. Instead, he stood back and watched as she bared her breast and rubbed her nipple across Beth's tiny mouth. Almost immediately she latched onto it and began sucking and making the funniest grunting noises.

Russell chuckled then eased onto the bed and wrapped his arms around them both. She eased back, letting him take their weight, enjoying the feeling of being safe and cared for. When she switched breasts, he blotted the free one dry for her. Then he nuzzled his mouth to her ear.

"I love you, Celina, and I love this tiny piece of heaven that you've given us. I will care for you both and keep you safe for as long as I live. If you'll let me, I'll be one of her fathers and she will be my child."

She gasped at his quiet proclamation. Her heart soared to hear him say the words, though she'd known them in her heart for weeks now. Turning her head, she reached for his mouth with her own. His kiss was gentle but no less passionate.

"I love you, Russell. Bethany and I would be honored for you and Abe to be her fathers. Nothing would please me more."

He all but crushed her to him as they watched their daughter slowly fall asleep in Celina's arms.

Chapter Sixteen

Six weeks later, Celina stepped out of the shower feeling refreshed with tiny sparks of excitement tingling up and down her spine. Tonight she was going to make sure her men made love to her. It had been plenty long enough. Her body was healed, and her hormones were screaming. She needed to feel them inside of her. They had been tiptoeing around her long enough.

Little Bethany was the sweetest baby. She still demanded feeding every three to four hours, but slept nearly nonstop in between. She rarely cried. As long as they kept her fed, warm, and dry, she was a happy baby. That made for a happy mom. Now to add satisfaction to the mix.

The men stayed busy from sunup to sundown preparing the garden then planting it as well as taking care of all the normal chores. It was time she took back over her part of the work, starting with taking care of them. With a small smile, Celina dressed in the only pretty dress she had found among the bunches of clothes now piled on one of the spare beds. She hadn't bothered with underwear.

She stopped to look once more in the mirror and sighed. Her breasts were much bigger than they had been, and though she'd managed to lose most of the weight she'd gained during her pregnancy, she still had a small rounded belly and her ass looked too broad. There was nothing she could do about it right now. In time she hoped the hard work of taking care of the garden and the house would help tone her body back in shape. She wanted to look her best for her men.

She hurried downstairs to check on Beth. Abe was watching her while he finished up dinner. The instant she walked into the kitchen, Abe turned to stare at her, forgetting the spoon he held in his hand until it dropped to the floor.

"Damn!" He leaned over and picked it up, dropping it in the sink before he stalked toward her. "You look good enough to eat."

"Promises, promises. I'm beginning to think you're all talk and no action." She pouted as he wrapped his arms around her.

"Baby, we don't want to hurt you. You just had a baby." He kissed her forehead.

"It's been six weeks, Abe! Six long, dry weeks. I'm ready for some action."

"I just want to be sure you're all healed up. I can't stand the idea of hurting you." He nuzzled her ear before nipping it and pulling away. "Dinner is almost ready. Have a seat. Russell should be in soon."

Just as she sat down, they heard the door in the great room open and close. Abe grabbed his rifle and checked to be sure it was Russell before relaxing and replacing the gun next to the cabinet. Russell strode into the room and made a beeline to where Bethany lay snug in her bed on a chair pushed up to the table for stability. He grinned down at her before turning to Celina.

"I see where your loyalties lie. I'm just second fiddle now, aren't I?" She gave a small pout and gazed up at him from beneath her lashes, hoping for a sexy look.

"Never, sweetness. You and Beth are my favorite women in the world." He bent over and kissed her with enough passion that Celina held some hope that her plan would work after all. "You look real pretty in that dress, Celina."

She smiled up at him and started to wrap her arms around his waist, but he stepped back.

"Not yet. I need a shower. I'm nasty. I'll hurry, though. I'm starved." He fairly ran out of the room.

Shaking her head, Celina smiled at Abe. She walked over and wrapped her arms around him from behind and rubbed her cheek against his back. He smelled so good. Warm, spicy male. Where Russell's scent had a slight pine smell to it, Abe's was more musky and earthy to her. Russell smelled more like a forest. She would know them by their scent alone.

Abe's hands covered hers as they reached in front of him. She couldn't completely encase him in her arms. He patted her hands.

"None of that, now. We're fixing to eat."

She could hear the amusement in his voice, but underneath it was a thread of heat as well. She wondered if she ran her hands downward if she'd find him hard or not. She was almost afraid to see. If he wasn't, it would hurt. Throwing caution to the wind, Celina slipped her hands down and found the object of her desire, long, thick, and hard.

"Celina." He groaned while pressing his cock against her questing hand.

Then he sighed and pulled her hands away from him. She let out a snort of disgust and started to back away but he stopped her, pulling her around to face him. He started to say something, but little Bethany chose that moment to decide she wanted attention. Celina stepped out of Abe's arms and hurried over to tend to the baby.

By the time Russell had returned and Abe had the food on the table, she had finished feeding her and was rocking her back to sleep.

"Looks like the little squirt ate first as usual," Russell said.

"Nothing but the best for our little girl." Abe passed the bowl of food to Russell after spooning some on Celina's plate.

"That's too much, Abe. I'll never eat all of that." She scowled at him as she carefully settled the baby back into her bed.

"You've got to keep up your strength. I don't want you losing any more weight. You're going to dry up and blow away if you do."

Russell nodded his head in agreement as he chewed. When he had swallowed, he spoke up.

"We like curves and meat on your bones so we aren't afraid of breaking you."

"Maybe if you were doing anything with me, I'd believe that. As it stands now, I wouldn't know what you mean." She didn't look up as she spoke.

The low growl on her right told her that Abe didn't like her pushing the subject. Well, too bad. She was tired of the frustration and needed her men to fuck her. She wanted them to make love to her, too, but some good old-fashioned screwing was what she needed first.

"Celina, honey. You're still healing…"

"Don't even try that. It's been six weeks. I'm freaking healed already." She glared at Russell then turned her irate gaze on Abe. "Either you start taking care of me or I'll take care of myself and leave you boys high and dry."

"She did not just threaten us," Abe said in a low almost guttural voice.

"I believe she did, friend." Russell had an amused expression on his face, but Abe's was quiet anger.

Celina shivered. What had she started? Maybe she should have tried being a little less aggressive after all. Though she wasn't really afraid, the intensity in Abe's eyes had her pussy clamping down as her juices gathered. Her stomach flip-flopped while her gut clenched.

"Finish your dinner, Celina. We have some things to talk about—upstairs." Abe watched her as he ate.

The feel of his eyes on her soon had her blood boiling and her pussy soft and wet. She shivered with the sensation of tiny fingers dancing down her spine. She snuck a glance over at Russell and licked her lips at the heat of his gaze as it slid over her straining breasts that threatened to spill out of the top of the low-cut dress she had on.

She had to make herself take each bite of food. All she could think about was what awaited her once they climbed the stairs later. This was what she'd been begging for all week. Finally, they would give her what she so desperately needed and wanted. The anticipation was killing her, and she was sure they knew it.

As soon as the table was cleared and the dishes put away, Abe picked up Beth's bed and nodded at Russell. She started toward the door that led into the great room, but Russell stopped her.

"Not yet. Abe is going to get Bethany settled. Strip for me."

"What? Here?" She looked around the room. They were in the kitchen, for goodness' sakes.

"Do as I said. Don't argue with me, Celina."

She started to do just that, but a little voice in the back of her head warned her not to screw up a good thing. She was going to get what she wanted in the long run if she played along. With only a few reservations, she slowly peeled her dress over her head and let it drop to the floor. Russell's indrawn breath sounded harsh in the quiet of the room. He burned her with his gaze as he dragged it down her body and back up again.

"You are the most beautiful woman, Celina. Looking at you is like looking at perfection."

She felt the heat of her blush crawl up her neck and face. He made her feel beautiful the way he talked to her. Both men were generous with their compliments, and it was good for her self-esteem.

"We better go upstairs before I take you on the kitchen table. As much as I'd like to, I think Abe has plans upstairs." Russell urged her toward the door.

When she turned to hurry through the door, he landed a quick slap to her ass that barely stung. She squealed because she knew he would appreciate it then hurried across the room to the stairs.

"Don't run up those stairs, or your ass will be too sore to sit down for a week."

She stopped and slowly climbed the steps ahead of him, making sure to swish her butt for good measure. The low groan behind her let her know she'd succeeded with her teasing. Her pussy juices slipped down her thighs as she stepped up on the landing. At this rate, she would be slick all the way down to her knees before they even touched her. Turning them on made her feel sexy and had her pussy hot and aching for something thick and hard to fill it.

Celina walked into the bedroom and froze. There were candles and lanterns all over the room. The soft scent of roses filled the air. Where had they found roses? Looking around, she didn't see any flowers so they must have found something that smelled of the delicate blooms. Abe stood to one side of the bed, wearing nothing but a pair of boxers. She could tell by the bulging material that he was ready. His eyes held arousal so fierce it was almost frightening.

She heard rustling behind her. She turned her head and found Russell pulling off his clothes as well. Her hungry eyes moved back and forth between them. She wanted to taste them and feel the pulsing of their thick cocks in her mouth.

Without thinking, she sank to her knees and reached for Abe's thigh with one hand. She looked up and licked her lips.

"Please. I need to taste you."

If it was possible, his face grew tighter as his eyes flashed. He lowered his boxers and stepped out of them before moving closer to her. One hand stroked the length of his long cock, squeezing at the base before pulling back up the thick stalk. His other hand reached out and cupped her cheek before pulling her forward so that her lips touched the tip where her tongue flicked out and seized the pearl of pre-cum that beaded there.

His hiss of breath was music to her ears even as she moaned at the tangy taste of him. She licked him from tip to base and back up again before sucking in the bulbous cap to tease with her tongue. His fingers dug into her scalp as if it was all he could do to hold on and not lose control. She loved the power it gave her over this mountain of a man. She reveled in the feel of his thighs quaking beneath her hand.

When she slipped one hand down to cup his swollen balls, he growled and pulled back.

"That's enough. I'll never last. I think Russell could use some attention, though." Abe spoke in a strained voice as he gently turned her toward the other man.

"Seeing you suck his cock almost had me shooting my load standing here. You're so fucking sexy." Russell ran his hand over her hair as she pulled his boxers down.

She smiled at the way his dick pulsed in her hand as she grasped him at the base. His hands rested on her shoulders as Abe pulled her hair back to watch. Celina smiled as she reached out with her tongue and licked around the cockhead before running it over the slit at the top filled with his cum. His salty taste exploded in her mouth. She hummed around him as she sucked him deep into her mouth. His curse had her fighting to keep from smiling as she wrapped her tongue around the stalk on her way back up.

Russell pulled her off of him with a groan. "You're going to be the death of me."

He and Abe helped her to her feet then pushed her toward the bed. She climbed up and crawled to the middle, where she lay back and watched them from beneath her lashes. They were amazing to look at. Tall, muscular, and sexy as hell, both men oozed confidence and strength through their pores. She had to be luckiest woman in the world.

Abe almost dove between her legs, stretching out on the bed so that he stared up her body at her. When he licked his lips and drew in her scent, all reason left her. She lifted her hips in silent invitation. He accepted it with one long lick down the center of her pussy. She sighed at the sensation of his tongue licking at her pussy lips before sucking first one then the other into his hot mouth.

Russell crawled across the bed and captured her mouth with his. He sipped at her lips before slipping his tongue between them and tangling with hers. He devoured her like a man starved before moving to her chin and then her ear. He suckled at her earlobe, nipping it twice then soothing it with a kiss.

As Russell slowly licked his way down her neck and across her chest, Abe drew circles around her throbbing clit with his tongue. He sucked on it then slipped two fingers inside her hot cunt. She moved her hips, hoping he would get the message that she needed more. Instead, he nipped her clit with his teeth and slowed his questing fingers until she wanted to scream. She knew better than to try to demand what she wanted. Abe liked to lead, but she couldn't help it. It seemed like she had been waiting forever for them to fuck her.

Slowly, Abe increased the speed of his thrusting fingers while lashing her clit with his tongue. With Russell's mouth sucking and nipping at one sensitive nipple and using his fingers to twist and tease the other, Celina was sure she would come soon. In spite of how tender her nipples were from breastfeeding, Russell seemed to know just how to manipulate them without making it painful. Instead the pleasure Abe was giving her pussy built on the torturous arousal Russell had created using her breasts. There was no way Celina would survive the coming explosion.

Out of the blue, Abe twisted his fingers and brushed over her sweet spot before clamping down on her clit with his lips and sucking the little button until spasms of pleasure shook her body. The orgasm flowed over her in one huge wave of bliss. She didn't even have time to scream as they wrung every drop of delight from her quivering body.

Even before she managed to totally regain her breath, Abe was urging her to straddle Russell's body and take his thick dick inside of her cunt. She sighed as he slowly filled her until she sat flush against his pelvis. Her clit brushed against his wiry pubic hairs, sending another shiver through her body.

She rose up and slowly dropped back down on him, enjoying the tightness around his mouth as he fought to remain in control. She wanted to take some of that control. With a small smile, she squeezed her cunt until he hissed out a breath and bucked beneath her.

"Too good. Hell, Abe. Do something to distract her. She's squeezing my dick like a fucking vise down here."

She laughed and started to do it again, but Abe slid a hand down her spine and pressed her forward until she was lying on top of Russell's chest. Abe ran his hands over her exposed ass cheeks, squeezing and massaging them as he spread them wide. Celina couldn't suppress her moan. She knew what was coming and couldn't wait to feel both of her men inside of her.

Russell began to rub his hands up and down her back, holding her still as Abe began to run a finger covered in something slippery up and down the crack of her ass. He stopped to ream her back hole before adding more of the slick stuff to her ass. She groaned when he slowly slipped a finger past the tight, resistant ring and began to pump it in and out of her. The deliciously naughty feeling sent shivers down her spine.

Abe continued to work first the one and then a second finger in and out of her tight back hole until she was pushing back, trying to fuck herself on his fingers. Russell held her hips still to prevent her from moving around too much. Frustration had her growling low in her throat and Abe chuckled at her.

"Your ass is so perfect, baby. I can't wait to sink my cock in this tight hole."

"Hurry, Abe. I can't stand it. I need you both inside of me." She knew she was whining, but she couldn't help it.

Need, hot and dark, pulsed through her bloodstream as Abe gave her dark rosette a few more pumps with his fingers before removing them. He added more of the homemade lube, and the next thing she felt was pressure as he pressed his slicked-up cock against her ass.

Chapter Seventeen

Abe felt as if he'd died and gone to heaven as he slowly pushed past the tight, resistant rings of Celina's ass. Nothing could ever compare to the feel of all that tight heat that enveloped him like a wet glove. Her low moans only added to his desire as he pulled back then sank deeper with each thrust of his dick. He gritted his teeth to keep from moving too fast. He didn't want to hurt her, and he was already holding on by a thin string of control.

"Oh, God, Abe. Please hurry. I'm dying." Celina's voice plucked at his control.

"Your sweet ass is so good, baby. I'll never last." Abe ground his teeth as he slowly sank deeper into her ass.

Each slow slide of his cock deeper into her back hole stole more and more of his control from him. His shaft felt as if it was on fire. When he was finally balls-deep in her ass, Abe sighed and rested his forehead at the small of her back then he kissed her and caught Russell's tortured gaze. They began moving in tandem. When he withdrew, Russell surged upward. They anchored Celina between them as they tunneled in and out of her sweet body. Abe had never felt anything half as good as this.

Sharing Celina with Russell meant more than just keeping Celina safe. It was sharing in her pleasure and knowing that between the two of them she would never know anything but happiness. It was watching the pleasure of her orgasms when before he would have missed them as he succumbed to his own. The beauty of her release stole his breath.

"Oh, hell, Abe. Get busy, man, or I'm never going to make it."

"She's fucking strangling me. I don't want to hurt her." Abe felt sweat slide down his back.

"You're not going to hurt me. Move, Abe! I need you to fuck me!" Celina's words seemed to be all he needed to release his control.

He slammed into her and groaned at the pure fire that danced down his cock and back up to the base of his spine. Over and over he pumped inside of her as Russell countered his moves beneath her. She moaned louder and began to shiver between them as her climax built between their bodies.

"Oh, God! Don't stop!" she screamed.

Abe felt his balls begin to tighten and bursts of fire gather at the base of his spine as he grew closer to coming. When Celina screamed and climaxed around them, her ass clamped down on his cock like a vise. He groaned and thrust twice more before his balls exploded and he filled her ass with his cum.

Russell's shout just after his let him know that his partner had reached his limit of Celina's tight cunt. He gasped for breath, trying not to lean too heavily on the two people below him. Finally he managed to slip from her delicious body and fall to the side. He smiled at the site of their woman sound asleep between them. After a few seconds more, he dragged himself off the bed and retrieved a warm, wet cloth to clean their woman up. As he wiped her body down, Abe thanked the good Lord for bringing both of them into his life. He couldn't imagine his life without them in it anymore.

"God, she's something special," Russell said as he twirled a tendril of her hair in his fingers.

"I know. All I want to do is keep her wrapped up in tissue paper where she's safe. This world is too dangerous for someone as sweet and loving as she is."

"She's a survivor, too, Abe. She'll fight for the ones she loves."

"I know. That's what scares me. I'm scared of losing her because she's so fierce. She'll sacrifice herself for little Bethany as well as for us. I'm terrified of losing her." Abe sighed as he stroked Celina's back.

"We'll keep her safe. That's part of our job and why there's two of us." Russell sighed. "Why was it so hard to think about sharing my first wife but the idea of not sharing Celina with you almost seems wrong?"

"You accepted that this is what it took to keep a woman safe," Abe said.

Russell didn't say anything more. After a few minutes, soft snores told Abe that his partner had drifted off to sleep. He figured Bethany would wake soon for her midnight feeding, so he might as well stay awake to get her. The thought of the little bundle of joy brought a smile to his face. She was a good baby. His heart swelled every time he thought about her. He couldn't wait to start teaching her all about the world around them. He'd teach her how to protect herself and how to live off the land so she would never go hungry.

About twenty minutes later, the sound of Beth snorting had him grinning like a loon as he slipped out of the bed and went to take care of his daughter. After cleaning her up and changing her diaper, Abe brought her back into the bedroom and eased Celina away from Russell so he could help her get situated to feed little Bethany.

"What is it?" Celina yawned.

"Time to feed Beth. Let's get you comfortable." Abe eased the covers down to her waist after propping her up with a pillow.

He carried Beth over and eased her into Celina's arms. He couldn't help but smile as Celina made a face when little Beth latched on to her nipple. He knew she would be tender after their play. He'd warned Russell to go easy on her.

"She's amazing," he said in a whisper.

"Isn't she, though? I can hardly believe that she was living inside of me all that time."

"You're a good mother, Celina. She's going to grow up to be a wonderful person."

"I love you, Abe." She reached out with one hand and touched his face with a smile.

"I love you, baby. You make me happy. I wasn't living until you and Russell came into my life."

"You can say that again," Russell said in a grumpy voice. "It took you long enough to smarten up, though."

"Smarten up about what?" Abe asked as the other man sat up next to Celina and made faces at little Beth.

"About how much better it is to have friends."

"And lovers," Celina added with a naughty twinkle in her eyes.

Abe reached over her and the baby to clasp Russell on the shoulder. "Thanks for not giving up on me, man. There's no one I would have ever wanted as my friend or at my back more than you."

"I owe you my life, because it allowed me to have a second chance at happiness." Russell kissed Celina lightly on the lips then bent and kissed little Bethany on her wrinkled forehead. "I love you both, Celina. You're my heart, and she's the light of my soul."

* * * *

Celina stared down at the two men who had changed her life after saving it as they lay sleeping in the bed. She had gotten up to use the bathroom and then checked on her precious Beth. After everything that had happened in her life, she finally felt as if her world was right. She had loved Roger with all her heart and would have gone on loving him, had he lived, but he was gone, and these two men had given her that second chance Russell had talked about.

The fact that they understood what it meant to lose a part of your heart had helped her come to terms with her own loss. Then they had shown her that it was okay to love again. She had no doubt that their lives would continue to be a struggle, but she knew she could depend on them to do their best and be there for her and Beth. Maybe one day they would have more children so she wouldn't grow up without other children around her.

She looked out the window into the starry night. Maybe others would find their way here and they could build a community where everyone looked out for everyone else. Whether that happened or not only time would tell, but until then, Celina planned to love her men with all her heart. She was truly content and happy in their love.

THE END

WWW.MARLAMONROE.COM

ABOUT THE AUTHOR

Marla Monroe has been writing professionally for about ten years now. Her first book with Siren was published in January of 2011. She loves to write and spends every spare minute either at the keyboard or reading another Siren author. She writes everything from sizzling hot contemporary cowboys, to science fiction ménages with the occasional bad-ass biker thrown in for good measure.

Marla lives in the southern US and works full time at a busy hospital. When not writing, she loves to travel, spend time with her cats, and read. She's always eager to try something new and especially enjoys the research for her books. She loves to hear from readers about what they are looking for next. You can reach Marla at themarlamonroe@yahoo.com or visit her website at www.marlamonroe.com.

For all titles by Marla Monroe, please visit
www.bookstrand.com/marla-monroe

Siren Publishing, Inc.
www.SirenPublishing.com